8/04

D0437346

Maata's
Journal

Maata's Journal

A NOVEL

PAUL SULLIVAN

ATHENEUM BOOKS FOR YOUNG READERS
New York London Toronto Sydney Singapore

ATHENEUM BOOKS FOR YOUNG READERS
An imprint of Simon & Schuster
Children's Publishing Division
1230 Avenue of the Americas
New York, New York 10020

Book design by Ann Sullivan
The text of this book is set in ACaslon.
Printed in the United States of America
First Edition
2   4   6   8   10   9   7   5   3   1

Library of Congress Cataloging-in-Publication Data
Sullivan, Paul, 1939–
Maata's journal / by Paul Sullivan.—1st ed.
p.   cm.
Summary: Stranded on an island during a mapping
expedition in 1924, a seventeen-year-old Inuit girl writes
about her life on the tundra and the changes brought about
by the Europeans who settled Canada.
ISBN 0-689-83463-2
1. Inuit—Juvenile fiction. [1. Inuit—Fiction.
2. Inuit—Fiction.] I. Title.
PZ7 .S95345 Tu 2003
[Fic]—dc21   99-44103

IN MEMORY OF

Anna K. Johnson

In the short northern summer of 1923, a small expedition was sent into the sub-Arctic just above the tree line. The party consisted of four men and a young Inuit girl. They were to map the area, record the weather, and study the geology. They were also to set up a permanent station on an island called Tumak.

Maata's Journal

chapter one

The snow stopped last night. I went to the far end of the island where it climbs high above the bay. The wind has piled the snow over the place where we had the fire. There were only a few black timbers pushing up out of the snow, with the ice on them sparkling in the sun. But the wind had taken all the snow off Olson's grave, sweeping the rocks clean. I piled on more rocks to keep the bears away from him.

When we came to the island there were five of us. Olson died two days after the fire. Nicolson

1

and Smith left for Seal Bay three months ago. When the day is clear I come and search from this high place with Morgan's field glasses. But there is never any sign of them returning, of a dog team or a human person. There is only the endless land. High and low ground covered with snow to the north and west, and to the east and south the frozen sea. Great ice ridges and floating cakes of thick ice. So thick and so tight, a person could walk easily over them. If I were returning from Seal Bay to this place with a dog team, I would come over the sea ice. I would have tried to reach there in the same way. But Nicolson and Smith went to the west, over the tundra, a very long way. They had an unspoken fear of the sea ice. But the sea ice is not shifting. Not moving. That will not happen for many weeks. So it could be traveled if a person knows to watch for open leads. But I believe there would not be many open leads.

My father would have known this and how to travel safely. Tiitaa, my brother, would know the same. But it is natural for the Inuit to know this in their own land.

I piled more stones on Olson's grave and spoke words in my mind from Morgan's Bible book. I think he is safe from the bears.

I took a long time returning to our little cabin because the sun was warm and good on my body. The sun warmed the surface of the snow, and I could hear the snow whisper to the sun. My people call the sun Hekenjuk. We believe she is the sister of the moon, Taktik. They share the same house but visit the sky at different times. There is always one coming when one is going away.

I lowered the hood of my parka and let my hair tumble over my shoulders. I think I would like to have a sunbonnet like the women in Quebec City. Only because it would be a nice thing for a girl to have. And when July comes and buttercups and purple saxifrage bloom on the tundra, I would cover my bonnet with little flowers. I could be a sassy thing and I could show off, though there is only Morgan.

Morgan was outside when I reached the cabin. I could see him sitting on the rocks as I came up from the bay. It is only the second time he has been outside since Nicolson and Smith left us. It is better for him to be outside. I have tried to tell him, but this he did on his own.

"You were gone a long time," he said.

"I went to the place where Olson is."

He said he was worried about me. That I must

be careful of the bears. There are too many bears now. And there was a seal on the ice. "The bears are hunting," he said.

"I know. You shouldn't worry."

"Yes. Of course you know. This is your land." And he asked if I kept a cartridge in the rifle.

I hesitated, lowering the heavy rifle from my shoulder. "No," I told him.

"Always keep a cartridge in the rifle. Here, see this? That is the safety. You put in a cartridge and push up the safety." Then he told me to try it.

I pulled the bolt back as I had learned, slipped in one of the long cartridges, and pushed the bolt forward. Then I pushed up the safety.

"Well done," he said. His voice was stern but not angry. Still, it was not the voice of the old Morgan. Then he showed me how to drop the safety down with my thumb when I was ready to fire. And again he told me to always keep a cartridge in the rifle. "Will you promise me?"

"Yes," I said.

He complained that he should have taught me to shoot. He didn't know things would go the way they had gone. His voice was a little angry now, but angry with himself. I tried to ease his mind, telling him no one could know all that would happen on Tumak Island. And I would have to learn to use the rifle.

He listened quietly. Then he asked me to help him back inside. He looked sad, with his beard long and his hair uncut and his eyes tired. I was surprised at how much weight he had lost when I helped him move back into the cabin. I could feel his bones against my shoulder. His hands had healed much since the fire, but his fingers were cramped and bent and he used them like claws. I helped him back on the cot, and he lay under the caribou skins. He had a little fever, but his fever comes and goes away. Today he was strong, but yesterday he was weak. Tomorrow, I don't know.

I made tea, but Morgan was sleeping when I brought the cup to him.

Later I melted snow to make water, and washed my hair and my body clean. I worked to finish my boots. And tonight I wrote in my journal.

April 27

My father was called Krakoluk. He was a great hunter and very much respected. He was not a big man, but small and powerful. He had a round face and dark happy eyes and thick black chin whiskers. I remember that his hands were big and strong and he could lift me, onto the *kamotik* or in play, with no effort. When he laughed it was like a roar, and others would fall into laughter with him. They caught his laughter because it was true and deep and endless.

Once, when I was small, I remember all the people followed my father to hunt caribou. We left our camp and traveled two days to a place of low hills and a narrow valley. In this place we waited several more days for the caribou herd to arrive. My father and the others appeared to know the deer would come this way. I remember the hunters gathering with bows and arrows and all of us, women and children, helping to build snares.

Then late one morning the herd arrived, flowing into the valley like a gray river on the white land. From the slopes of the hills, the hunters rained down arrows while at the end of the valley women and children drove the herd into the snares. There was great excitement and commotion, with the deer struggling frantically to break free. Everything was happening so fast, with the deer rushing by and loose snow kicked into the air and the shouts and cries of the people. I became frightened and confused, running with the deer and crying, like the deer trying to break free. But I could not free myself of the running herd and sea of antlers. Then I felt the strong hand of my father lift me from the ground and tuck me up under his arm.

He carried me to the place where my mother and other women were busy dressing out the deer, and there he dropped me. And then quickly, he had gone back into the hunt. And there I sat crying and ignored by the women. I was no longer frightened but felt anger at being ignored, and I cried louder and louder until Tiitaa came and took me by the hand. After that my crying stopped.

The women were at work butchering the kill, cutting up the meat and sharing it out, loading it on the *kamotiks* where it would freeze quickly. The caribou skin was carefully removed. Sinew was cut from the legs. And with stones, the bones were crushed and the marrow removed and placed in the stomach of the deer to be carried away.

Tiitaa found a large stone for me to use and showed me how to hammer and split the bones and pull out the long ropes of sweet marrow. Then Tiitaa went away to join my father in the hunt, and all that day I worked beside my mother. My mother worked silently and skillfully, with her eyes at times shifting to me. If I pushed aside a piece of bone not properly cleaned, she would place it before me again, split it open, and show me what I had missed. But my mother always did this with a smile. We worked long that day. Until snow shadows formed and our *kamotiks* were full and the teams could pull no more. Until the sun was going away and put a copper light on the soft brown face of my mother. And I remember her smile and the wind blowing through the fur of her parka. And her hair long and black like my hair. I remember that from my beginning.

There was a feast when we returned from the hunt that lasted deep into the night. There were games, and stories were told, and my father danced about the floor with the skin drum. My father shouted in a loud song voice when he was dancing to the drum, bringing his feet down heavy on the floor, rolling his body like a bear. Tiitaa took up a pair of caribou antlers and held them to his head. He took up the dance. When I started laughing he came at me and chased me about the room. I tried to escape but could find no place to hide until I found the arms of my mother, and there she held me safe from Tiitaa. And there I stayed until sleep came.

In that time all of the meat from the hunt was shared out to each family. And all worked evenly and for long hours into the winter darkness. And the men would go out again and again, if there were no storms, to hunt seal and caribou and catch fish through the ice. The men followed my father. And my mother, who was called Nua, appeared to be at the center of all the women in our small band. And life was good to us in this land others call harsh.

April 28

Today I practiced with the rifle again. I set an old biscuit tin up on the rocks for a target. And I lay on my belly in the snow, taking aim with the rifle. And I hit it! *Smack!* And the tin went up in the air. Way up in the air. And I got up dancing. I shot the tin two times using three cartridges. But the first shot was the best time. On the first shot I hit it. *Smack!*

When I came back to the cabin, Morgan was a little angry. He heard the rifle shots and it worried him. He thought maybe I had met a bear. I told him I shot a biscuit tin two times. He said nothing. But I know he was annoyed.

Morgan is right about the bears. I saw two bears this morning going to my traps. There are a lot of bears now. Maybe they favor this island as a seal-hunting place.

There didn't appear to be so many bears when we first arrived here. There was little of anything on the island then. It was July of last year when the supply ship dropped us here. When the bay was free of ice. We spent the first day unloading our supplies from the small boats that brought them to shore. Carrying the stuff far up on the rocky beach. The island was bare of snow and ice then. And cotton grass, Arctic poppies, and heather covered the slopes. Hundreds of noisy gulls nested in the rocks, and on the far side of the island was a colony of snow geese.

Morgan and Olson and I went off to explore the island on the second day, walking the full length of it along the shore and then back over the high ground. Morgan selected the place for the cabin and made careful notes and drawings in his book. I went off into the rocks, searching for gulls' eggs. When I brought the eggs back and offered them to Olson, he just tightened up his face and turned away. "No, thanks," he said. "I'll have to be close to starvation before I'll start on raw birds' eggs."

So I ate them myself, punching a small hole in each and holding it to my lips to suck it dry.

"The girl is still half wild," Olson told Morgan. "That school in Quebec did nothing for her."

Morgan just laughed and rested his hand on Olson's big shoulder. "Yes. And it's the wild half we'll need here," he told him.

Olson was Morgan's good friend and had been with him for many years. The first time Morgan came to our settlement, Olson was with him. Olson frightened me badly, for I was only a small girl and he seemed a giant. He appeared very high above me, and his arms hung long down his sides. His head was big and his neck thick around. He was bigger than Morgan, who was bigger than my father. And when he pulled back the hood of his parka, he had no hair. His head was completely smooth. A polished round top, red from the sun and wind off the tundra. And he had a long red mustache that curved far down each side of his mouth, so when he smiled it framed his big white teeth.

At that time he frightened me, and I stayed close to Tiitaa. But Olson, I would learn, was a soft-spoken, gentle man. And one who would even scold me years later for stealing eggs from the gulls nesting in the rocks. He was uneasy at seeing the nest invaded by an Inuit girl who had no real hunger. But I was fond of gulls' eggs and went back again and again.

It makes me sad now to write about Olson because I grew to love him as a friend. And to the man who frightened me so as a child, I would owe much. It always happened that he was my protector when Tiitaa wasn't around.

I can cook and I can sew. This is part of the reason why Morgan brought me on the expedition. And because I read and write English very well Morgan also encouraged me to keep a journal. Olson agreed that I might be an asset. That I might brighten the dark months of the northern winter. But Smith and Nicolson were against my coming. I had to prove myself to both, though Smith was the more difficult from the beginning.

Smith saw no need for some Eskimo girl to come along, and he openly complained to Morgan about it. But Morgan cut Smith short, telling him they had come to work.

"Our time will be given to mapping the island and the coast," Morgan said. "Maata can take some of the chores from us."

They would have only a few months of daylight

before the winter darkness, he told Smith. And a short time after, before the supply ship came in July. July was the only time the bay would be free of ice.

So Smith fell quiet about my coming along. But in his moody way he continued to show his disapproval.

Nicolson said nothing. He just ignored me most of the time. He wasn't dark and gloomy like Smith. He didn't have Smith's sullen nature. He kept quietly to himself, working on his charts in the light of the lamp or out running the team for days at a time. Nicolson was good with the dogs. Morgan respected him for that and let the team fall to his care. But he had a real fear of the sea ice. He would cross the narrow channel when it was frozen over, but he would not venture out onto the frozen sea. I think he had heard too many stories of the ice breaking up and people being stranded on a floe. There are a lot of stories like that. And many of them true. Many men have drifted away on the black water and never returned.

Smith and Nicolson were not alike, though both were small in build, not as tall as Morgan and nothing near the height of Olson. Nicolson had a thick crop of dark hair and a round, powerful body. In his parka, if his skin were not so light, he could have passed for Inuit. He had that short, strong build of my people. Smith was the same height but not as strong in build. And Smith's hair was thin and brown in color. He wore glasses most of the time and had a habit of cleaning them when he was talking, usually complaining about one thing or another. He was always worried and so always seemed to have a long list of things to complain about. I think Morgan wished he had never brought Smith along. And I learned that Nicolson had been with Smith on a previous expedition and disliked him openly.

The first thing we did after scouting the island was to build our cabin. Nicolson used the dog team to haul the wood and supplies up to the place Morgan had selected. They started the walls with stone, almost shoulder high, and finished the walls and roof with the lumber we had brought with us. I showed them how my father used moss between the stones and how he would cover the roof with moss and sand. And I showed them how my father would build a small front room that was lower than the main room as a place to enter. This would help keep the cold out, for cold air is heavy and does not rise easily. And there we would keep our winter gear and I would do the cooking.

Morgan liked the idea and the cabin was built in that way, and I knew that when the first snow covered it we would be warm and comfortable. Morgan was careful to try to build the cabin as solidly as possible. It had to serve as our only shelter until the ship returned the following year. And the place was to serve from then on as a station for other teams sent up to map and explore this part of the Arctic. The land was not new to my people, the Inuit, but much of it was unknown land to the government in Ottawa.

While the men worked on the cabin, Morgan gave me the task of collecting all the driftwood I could find around the island. We were just above the tree line, and little vegetation grew to any height in the thin topsoil of the tundra. While in the short weeks of summer the island comes alive with color from plants like the Arctic willow and rhododendron, which hold close to the earth, their roots cannot break through the permafrost. They grow as dwarfed plants huddling on the rocks. But on an island such as ours, there is always driftwood to be found. And I spent many days, after cooking for the men, going out to bring back all the driftwood I could gather. By the time the cabin was ready, I had brought in a good supply.

Morgan was impressed with the pile I had built up. Olson complimented me. Even Nicolson said, "Good job . . ." the only compliment he ever offered me.

Smith simply looked at the pile of driftwood briefly, adjusted the glasses on his nose, and walked away.

The men started to work as soon as the cabin was finished. They would be gone for days at a time. Morgan and Olson made up a team exploring the coast to the south. Smith and Nicolson made up the second team exploring to the north. They had the full use of the sun, for Hekenjuk never fell below the horizon. But after September Hekenjuk would slowly slip away. And by December we would be locked in a winter darkness that would last many weeks.

Morgan wanted much work finished before the darkness came. So for me the island often became a lonely place. In Inuktitut, the language of my people, the word for such a loneliness is *tumak*. When I told this to Morgan he named the island on his maps Tumak Island. And Olson named the channel after his wife back in Montreal, Jacqueline's Channel. And so it went with their work through those weeks of the long days. Until the first slushy ice started to appear on the surface of the sea. Until the first hours of darkness broke Hekenjuk's endless drifting. Then the first hard snows fell, and with the dog team, the men were gone an even greater time than before.

All of this happened when things were going well. Before the fierce winter storms and before the fire. And with this, Morgan was pleased. But none of us knew of the time to come.

This evening I trimmed Morgan's beard and his hair and washed him. Washing him, I saw a faint yellow color to his skin. He knew I saw it but said nothing. And there was a slight swelling in his feet and ankles. I think these are the first signs of scurvy, and he knows this. He has had nothing to eat but meat for many months now. And though it is warm in the cabin, it is always damp. All bad things for him. And it will be many weeks before the ship returns.

Tonight there is a hard wind across Tumak Island. And once again I write in my journal.

The corners of my journal are singed from the fire. If my journal hadn't been with Morgan's maps and papers Olson would not have saved it. Now, each time I open it, I remember.

chapter two

~ *May 1, 1924* ~

When I was a small child we moved freely from place to place, with our dog teams carrying all we owned on our sleds. There was a time, I was told, when we Inuit believed we were the only people in the world. And all of the world was like our world of ice and snow.

We hunted for caribou and seal. We fished for salmon trout and char. We gathered birds' eggs and bilberries and crowberries in the autumn. And we made our clothes of the skins of the animals we killed. We were happy and we didn't know any

18

differently. We didn't know until the strangers came and told us so.

First the strangers came for our furs and ivory. Often they took away our women. Then they came for our souls, giving us a new religion. Then they told us our world of ice and snow was not our world but belonged to the government in the south. It belonged to people who had never even seen it. Then they said that government would take care of us. But we didn't ask. We didn't know to ask.

When the weather grew warmer we all moved from our winter camp to our spring campsite. From that place my father and others made a trip over the ice before the breakup to the place where the strangers lived. They went to trade the furs they had collected that winter. It was a trip the men made almost every spring, and they were gone for days at a time. Gone to trade the fur of the white fox for tea and tobacco. And cartridges for those few who had guns. For steel knives and hatchets and often for sweet sugar candy. I remember the sugar candy and how we children waited, hoping, watching for the teams to return over the sea ice. Running out to meet them when they came. And how the camp would come alive with excitement when they did return. But that year, under the excitement, ran a strange uneasiness. It was written on the worn face of my father and others when they returned. It was unspoken but it was there, and even we children could feel it. Then one evening, when all of the people had gathered together, my father got up to speak. In a soft voice he announced that soon we all would be leaving. That we would abandon our spring camp for a new place. And though a quiet fell over the people, none appeared surprised. It was as if they already knew and accepted.

"When the ice is gone a ship will come," my father said. "At that time we must all be ready to leave. Each family must prepare."

We were being relocated by the government in the south. Our little band, and others, were to be taken off the land to live in a settlement. We would no longer be free to follow the seasons across the tundra. I didn't know this. And I waited with the excitement of a child for the time when the ship would arrive. But even then I knew something was wrong. For there were no drum songs. There was little laughter. It was as if the life had gone out of the people. My father became silent and withdrawn. My brother, Tiitaa, always angry.

And my mother and the other women no longer went out to search for eggs and berries or spent long hours working and sewing the skins for winter clothes as they had in the past.

I knew nothing of the place where we were going. In my child's mind it was surrounded by mountains of sugar candy. I was told that the Qallunaat, the whites who lived there, spoke a different language. And that the ship that would take us away was a hundred times the size of my father's small kayak. I was ready for the adventure. But my enthusiasm was not shared by others.

"This Inuk will not be taught the ways of the Qallunaat," Tiitaa said angrily. "The tundra is my home. It will always be my home."

"It is not a choice," my father said. And he told my brother we must do what the Qallunaat tell us. For they are powerful and we must live by their laws.

"They do not understand our ways."

"That is true. But we must do as we are told."

Tiitaa argued with my father.

Then my mother spoke firmly to Tiitaa. Her voice was cold and sharp, and I remember her words. "You will talk no more of this. You will frighten Maata. And the choice is not yours. The world of the Qallunaat is all around us. It will be upon you all of your life. And all of Maata's life."

So Tiitaa fell silent.

But Tiitaa knew the world of the strangers. He had gone with my father to trade the furs of the fox. He had seen this place, this settlement, perched on the edge of the bay. He had seen the low wood houses with the thin smoke pouring from their chimneys. And he knew the faces of the Inuit who had settled there. Who bought their goods from the Hudson's Bay Company store. Who attended the government school and mission church. Who took Christian names. Who sold carvings of stone and ivory to the south to buy tea and sugar candy. And who hunted only when the government allowed. My father always said they were not Inutuinnait, true Inuit. And this Tiitaa could not accept. We started to lose Tiitaa even before the great ship came to take us away.

My brother's anger put caution in me. But still, I took to the adventure. My mother began gathering up those items she would take on the journey. But it was not like before. She appeared uncertain. Always she had been so exact. Never a hesitation. Now she would look at me and smile as if waiting for me to answer. "Should I take this? Should I take that? Yes, I will certainly need my sewing needles. And woman's knife. The best warm clothes we will take. But how much will they allow us?"

I had seen my mother and the other women close down a camp in a few hours and load all they owned on *kamotiks*. They would travel for days across the open tundra in the worst weather and at a new campsite have the sleds unloaded and food waiting for us. But this was so different for her and all the women. Yet, for me, she always smiled and looked so positive. "It is a different thing," she whispered. "A way you do not know. But you will find good in it. You must always see with your eyes and not close them to different things. And you must always learn with your mind."

The old ways of the Inuit were disappearing, Mother explained. My world would always be influenced by the whites. I must survive in that world, not fighting the changes as Tiitaa would, or accepting in silence as my father would, but by taking what came and learning from the experience.

"In this you will be free," she told me. "You will always be Inuit. And you will always be my Maata."

May 5

Morgan gave me his old hat. He did not exactly give it to me. But he saw it on my head and said nothing. So now I am wearing it.

It is an old hat but good. It has a very wide brim to shade the sun from my eyes, and when summer comes I will cover it with flowers like a bonnet.

My new boots fit very comfortably and keep the water away. The snow was soft today and the sun warm. But my new boots are good boots. Each stitch was made close and tight.

Last night I thought I heard the ice shifting in the bay. I woke from my sleeping place and opened the door and went out in the night to listen. But I think it was my mind. It is much too soon for the ice to move. Taktik, the moon, was large and bright far out over the bay, and there was a little cold wind. I listened for a long time, but there was nothing. When I returned to my sleeping place, I could not sleep. I thought for a long time about the beginning. I thought a lot about my mother, and I missed her much. I missed her quiet strength and her gentleness. The way I always felt safe in her smile.

I am careful to have only one cup of tea in the morning now. I am saving the last tin for Morgan. He eats little food. He has had nothing for several days. And he becomes weaker each day. I am greatly worried for him.

May 6

The sun stays longer now and is warm. Soon I will take in my traps. I worked hard all this day cleaning and stretching fox skins. The sun was so warm, I took Morgan outside, and he sat for a long time looking away at the bay. I think the sun is good for him. His face is so hollow and thin. When a little wind came I covered his legs with a blanket. I took his old canvas coat to cover his shoulders, but he pushed it away. Two times he pushed it away. In the deep pocket of his coat, I found his pipe. So I put on his, my, hat. His coat. And with his pipe in my mouth, I paraded back and forth like a Qallunaaq. Just a little arrogant and trying to pull my feet out of the snow. It is the first time Morgan has laughed in a long time. And it was real laughter. And soon I was laughing. I fell in the snow laughing. And Morgan had tears in his eyes laughing. He was just like the old

Morgan. The only Qallunaaq who was Tiitaa's friend. And my friend always.

This evening Morgan asked me to bring him a leather case that held some of his maps. A case singed by the fire, with maps he and Olson had worked on. He spread a map out and on it showed me Tumak Island and a long way off, Seal Bay.

"I think the ice is still solid enough," he said. "You could walk out." He said it would not be easy. But he believed I could do it.

I looked at him quietly, a little confused. "But you are too weak."

He shook his head at me. "I would not be going. Only you."

"I will not leave you."

"Only you," he insisted. And he said he had no reason to think Smith and Nicolson ever made it to Seal Bay. And there was no good reason for me to stay here.

Once more I told him I would not leave him.

He looked angry. Again he shook his head. "Maybe I don't want you to stay here," he told me.

I must have looked hurt because his eyes were a little sad then. "You take the rifle," he said. "Leave the shotgun with me. Listen to me, Maata. Just go."

"The ship will come," I said.

"The ship will not come for weeks. And it may not come then. I don't want you here to watch me die!"

I took the map from him, folded it poorly, and stuck it back in the leather case. I would not talk of such a stupid thing. I told him I wouldn't talk about it anymore.

"I should never have brought you," he told me. And after that he fell silent.

"You will not die if you want to live." And then I added the one thing that did make him angry: "And I think you do not care if you live. I think you want to die because Olson is dead. But you did not kill Olson."

I could see the anger in his eyes and in the tight lock of his jaw. "Olson went back in the fire for the maps. If not for me, he wouldn't have gone. He would be here now."

"He went on his own."

"Not true," he said firmly. And he turned away, ending the conversation.

It is true that Olson died going back for the maps. Trying to save all the work they had done over the many months. Why this was so important I do not understand. But it was important to my gentle Olson, just as it was to Morgan. But Morgan was in charge, and Olson was his very best friend. So Morgan takes responsibility for all, and most of all for his friend.

May 7

The ice stays firm on the bay, but still the sun is warm on the snow. It is cold when there is a wind but not winter cold. I have done away with my heavy parka and wear Morgan's old canvas coat and his wide hat. I made a new case for his knife and a new strap for his field glasses. I have taken my traps in.

On this day I found much blood on the bay ice where a big bear killed a seal. I carry the rifle on the strap over my shoulder, with one cartridge in the chamber and the safety up. I practiced with the rifle to bring it to my shoulder and take off the safety, but I am very clumsy. And bears are very fast. I hope I must never face a bear in the open.

I walked across the island to the channel side. It is all new after the last snow. Looking through the glasses, I could see brown hills far away and places where the wind has blown the snow clean. They go for a long way, and Smith and Nicolson must have crossed them in the darkness of winter. I wonder how far they got from Tumak? Or how close they came to Seal Bay? If they lay frozen now on the far side of the hills?

I wish I had a good team of dogs. If I had a good team of dogs, I would cross the channel ice and travel far out to the brown hills to see what lies beyond them. I might even make it as far as Seal Bay.

No. I would run across the sea ice to Seal Bay. I think that can still be done. I would put Morgan on the *kamotik* under the blankets and run fast over the hard blue ice. Running like the wind, with the dogs pulling tight on the traces. Free of Tumak Island, and Morgan would not die because he would not have time to die. I would do that if I had a fast team. But I have nothing.

I saw a flock of geese far out over the tundra. I sat and watched them. A thin line very high and moving north. Too far away to hear them. Just silent motion. I sat in the snow watching until I could no longer see them. Not even with the glasses. When I returned to the cabin I told Morgan about the geese, but he looked doubtful. "Too soon," he said.

"No," I told him. "They are coming north again. And the sun stays longer now."

He said nothing, letting it pass away from him.

But I wanted to push it, trying to cheer him up. "And if we see the geese, maybe the ice will clear early and the ship will come. Maybe the *Venture*. The *Venture* is a good ship. A strong ship."

"They will not send the *Venture*," he said quietly. "You know that, Maata. We are scheduled to be picked up by the *North Wind*, the Bay Company ship, when it passes in July. If the bay is clear of ice in July."

"They will send the *Venture*," I said.

"No, Maata. It will not happen that way." And he rolled up under the blanket as if ready to sleep.

So I still wish that they would send the *Venture*. But I know in my heart they will not do that. They will send the *North Wind*. A ship not so big and strong. And the *North Wind* will not challenge the heavy ice.

Once I thought the *North Wind* a great ship. I can remember the day, when I was a child, that it came into the bay to take us from the camp to the settlement. I remember the smoke pouring from its stack as it moved like a monster through the dark Arctic waters. And I remember the boats lowering from the side and the men working the oars to reach our rocky beach. Even the boats it dropped into the water were larger than my father's kayak. The *North Wind* was larger than a thousand kayaks. I stood fixed with wonder as the people came down to the water to help the men pulling in the boats. And beyond, between the sky and the sea, the *North Wind* waited like a big rusting island. Waiting silent and gray.

It all happened so suddenly that day. First the ship was on the horizon, and then it was in the bay. Then the small boats were there, with the rough faces of the sailors. The first Qallunaat I had ever seen. Big and almost angry-looking. Wet from the sea. Impatient with the people gathering around them. Talking in a language I had no understanding of. The sea was still running off their boats when they began loading us like cargo. Women, children, dogs, all tossed into the boats. Some ran back to their summer tents to gather what belongings they could carry in their arms. Mothers searched for their children and hunters for their families. And behind this confusion all were herded by the sailors toward the waiting boats.

One sailor grabbed me and lifted me into the air, and my excitement turned to fear. I started screaming and kicking as he passed me into the hands of another. When they dropped me into the boat, I tried immediately to climb out again, but I could not lift myself over. Then I felt a hand comfort me, one of my mother's sisters, but still I cried, lifting up on my toes to peer out over the side.

Back on shore the wind blew against our summer tents, and smoke still lifted below the drying racks. The sailors were going from tent to tent, pushing the people toward the beach. Rushing them like seals toward the water. Dogs snapped at the air or growled threats. Sled dog attacked sled dog over old angers. With no hunters to control them, they tore at one another savagely. Men argued in Inuktitut with sailors who ignored them totally while their women moved with panicked faces toward the boats. And tears washed down my face.

We all knew the ship was coming, but no one expected it to appear so suddenly and for us to be herded away with so little notice. That morning our camp had been full and life normal and a few hours later, empty with a few stray dogs that had not been taken on the boats. Our boat was pushed off into the water as were the others, and I could feel us lifting over the waves. As we moved away I looked back at the lonely place that had been our summer camp, with the empty tents and the sweep of tundra filled with July flowers, and I cried for my mother. Some of the boats had already made several trips to the *North Wind,* and I had no way of knowing that our boat was making the last and that she was waiting anxiously for me. That my father was with her. And that Tiitaa was in another boat only a short distance from me, for he had refused to leave until they forced him at the very end.

And so we left our camp way of life on the tundra. And the *North Wind* gathered us up like cargo. I can still hear the sound as the boats were lifted on the ropes up her iron side and we were hauled out. People, dogs, and bundles. All piled on the slippery deck in confusion. The Qallunaat passing through and shouting orders few understood. Pushing the women and children to one side and the men to another. I remember my first smell of dirty oil and rust and looking up to see the smoke pouring from the stack to stain the sky above. And I remember feeling the beating heart of the *North Wind,* the engines below, like some sad living thing.

My mother found me and took me in her arms. Then they moved us toward a doorway and down steep metal stairs. There was little light and the stairs narrow, and I clung to her hand. They moved all of us, all the women and children, down into this place, and we found others already there, other Inuit from other camps along the coast. A hatch was open above, and the light streamed down on their faces as they came out of the shadows. The look of them frightened me as much as the beating heart of the *North Wind.* They looked forlorn. Lost. And when they came close I saw the hair on their heads had been clipped almost to the flesh. The women and even the children in their arms. They came forward and there was an odd moment of silence, and then they reached out to greet us. They reached out, understanding our confusion and fear.

The ship was rocking like thin ice on a rough sea, and we made our way back to a corner, where Mother dropped the bundle that hung from her shoulder. In this way she claimed the place as our sleeping place. And there we settled near a woman with a small baby. The baby was sucking at the woman's breast, and she was cradling the head in her open hand. She spoke to us in a soft, comforting way. I moved far back in the corner, using my mother as my shield and pulling close the bundle as if it were a wall to hide behind. I do not remember what the woman said, or even if I was listening, but I remember my eyes fixed on her bare head. And after a time she smiled softly and looked at me. With her free hand she brushed over her head. "Lice," she said. I huddled back and away. "The Qallunaat have a great fear of lice. They found some, so they shaved the heads of all of us. But it is not such a terrible thing. The hair will grow back. It grows back now," she added, again brushing her head.

But still I could not help but look, for I had never seen a woman with no hair. And the thought of losing my long beautiful hair was too much for me. I looked at Mother, and she reached over to squeeze my hand.

Suddenly the heart of the *North Wind* began to beat loudly. I could feel it in the iron walls and vibrating against the floor. We were starting to move.

We were all quiet a moment. Looking up through the opening to the sky, I could see the smoke trailing back. A sense of motion gathered about us.

The woman told us she had been on the *North Wind* for six days. The first stop had been at their camp. But then the ship had made another stop before this one. And there was talk of still another stop before we would reach the place called

Foster's Bay and the new settlement. But she was not sure about these things, for she did not speak the language of the Qallunaat. "But the old one over there understands it," she said. And she looked toward an old woman who sat with a blanket pulled up over her thin legs. The old woman's head, like the others, had been shaved, but now a stubble of white was growing back against the brown of her skin. Her face was wrinkled and dry and the color of earth. As a young girl, we were told, she was taken from her village and made to stay two summers on a whaling boat and serve the men. She was made their whore. She hates the Qallunaat, but she understands much.

My mother was quiet, thinking, and again she squeezed my hand gently. "She must teach Maata," she said.

The woman wiped milk from the child's cheek and again took it to her breast. "I see no good in learning the language of the white people. Or any of the Qallunaat ways." And her daughter, she told Mother, would be raised to be Inutuinnait. True Inuit.

"You will raise your child," Mother said softly. "But she will be as the world around her. And we are no longer the only people."

The woman looked annoyed at us, pulled the infant closer to her breast, and turned her shoulders slightly away.

Mother opened the bundle that had been my safe wall. The outside of the bundle was a caribou-skin blanket. She used the blanket to cover the two of us, pulling me tight against her. I sat there quietly, my heart beating to the rhythm of the *North Wind*'s heart, watching the smoke move above the opening. Suddenly I thought of sugar candy, but just as suddenly the thought went out of my mind. I pushed closer to my mother and closer still.

May 9

I still allow myself only one cup of tea in the morning. I am saving most of the tin for Morgan. But Morgan has not drunk tea in several days, so I have given myself one extra cup this evening.

We were two weeks on the *North Wind*, pushing through the cold Arctic waters and the few ice floes that lingered. And we made three other stops along the coast at small camps. In the beginning I stayed close to my mother, but she had taken time to make friends with the old woman who spoke the language of the strangers. We moved our sleeping place close to hers, and she appeared to be pleased with the company. She was even older than I first thought her to be, and she was very ill. But her mind was sharp and clear. "I have lived more winters than a woman deserves," she told us. "I will not live another."

Mother offered to share our food and blankets with her, but she humbly declined, saying she ate almost nothing now and suffered from the dampness no matter how many blankets covered her old body.

Mother looked at her with understanding. "I am a woman who owns little things. Not important things. But I have fine sewing needles and a good knife. I would give you these things."

"And why would you give me these things?"

"If you would please teach my daughter the language the white people speak. I was told you know this."

The old woman studied me easily. She told Mother that she had no need for needles or an *ulu*. She held up her shaking hands, asking how they could hold a needle or a woman's knife. And she was not a teacher, she said. She knew only a little of the language.

"But a little is a beginning," my mother said.

The woman nodded her head, her eyes still on me, then she turned to Mother. "I will think about it," she offered. And she let us know it was not a language she found pleasure in.

"I understand," Mother said.

On the second day at sea a crewman cleared an area and set down a small table and two chairs. A short time later a woman appeared. She carried a board to which was clipped a thick stack of papers. She looked at us all seriously and started leafing through the papers. As she was doing this, a man dressed in white came down the iron stairs and took a chair behind the table. He was small of build with a sharp face, glasses, and a thin mustache. The woman passed him the board, and he sat reading through the papers. After a long time he finally looked up at us a little annoyed, as if we were all a great nuisance. Then he spoke to the woman in English as he wrote across one of the papers with a hurried hand. She turned to face us. Then she pointed to one near the table. It was Lisi, my mother's sister. The woman motioned for Lisi to come forward, and Lisi did this reluctantly.

Huddled close to Mother, I watched as the man came up to examine Lisi. First he looked in her mouth, forcing her mouth open wide and her head back. Then he felt about her neck with his fingers. He looked in her ears. Then her eyes. Then he listened to her breathing. As he was doing this, he was speaking and the woman was writing on the paper. Lisi appeared very nervous. When he was finished he turned to his assistant and nodded. Lisi relaxed, or at least seemed not so nervous as before. But then the woman stepped up, took her hand to the back of Lisi's head, and lowered it. Slowly she separated Lisi's long black hair. She seemed to take a long time going through Lisi's hair. Finally she nodded. The man said something, and the assistant placed Lisi in the chair, took up a large pair of scissors, and started clipping away at Lisi's long hair.

I watched in horror as lengths of Lisi's hair tumbled to the floor. The woman handled her brutally, turning her head one way and pushing it another, all the time the sound of the scissors filling the room even above the pounding heart of the *North Wind*, filling the silence that was us. And I could see Lisi's eyes shifting over us in embarrassment, searching our faces and turning away. And when it was over Lisi hurried off to her sleeping place with her head lowered.

Four others followed Lisi, and all received the same treatment. A quick examination, then placed into the chair and their hair clipped away. After this the woman swept all the hair into a neat pile on the floor. Then she turned and motioned to me. I held tight to my mother's arm; but Mother pulled my hand away and stood up. "I will go first," she told me. "You will see that it is not so bad."

I watched as my mother was examined and placed into the chair. The old woman we shared our sleeping place with whispered to me, "The Qallunaaq woman is enjoying this. She finds lice even when there are none."

As I watched my mother's hair fall to the floor, I curled the ends of my own black hair in my fingers nervously. When her eyes shifted over they were wide and looked at us proudly. And when she left the chair she walked just as proudly, with her head up, back to where I was waiting.

It was my turn, and I could feel my body shaking as I moved through the people and stood before the table. The man examined me roughly, twisting my head on my neck to look in my ears and into my eyes. I was staring into his thick glasses. He spoke to the woman, and she made quick notes on the paper. Then he returned to his chair behind the table. Then the assistant lowered my head to search for lice. She motioned for me to take the chair as she reached for the scissors. I took one quick look at the chair and the neat pile of beautiful black hair on the floor, and I bolted away. The woman turned in amazement. The man got up and leaned over the table, shouting at her. And I was gone.

I do believe they expected me to be taken by my own people and sent back. But a very different thing happened. With the woman chasing me, I took shelter in the crowd, and the people gathered in close, causing her to squeeze through angrily. I could see the smiles on the Inuit faces and hear the quiet laughter. And I could hear the woman threatening me as she pressed her way through. First in one direction and then another, only to have me slip away again. The man joined in the chase but showed little enthusiasm and less energy. He tried to block me to the right and left, but I slipped under his arms and made my way to the stairs. I raced up the iron stairs to the open deck, with the woman close behind, past two sailors who turned with laughter when they saw what was happening. Laughing at the woman who stumbled over a coil of twisted rope as she reached for me. And soon all those working on deck stopped to watch the chase.

I hid behind barrels and crates. I even used the sailors as shields. And none threatened or tried to hold me. And still she came. Her face red with anger, so close at times I could hear her breathing. But always I slipped away from her. Just out of reach. All of the crew was gathering on the deck to watch, and their laughter grew louder. And then I stumbled and went rolling over the deck. She would have got me then, but suddenly I was swooped up weightless in the big hands of a seaman, and I was being passed over the heads of the crew. I was swung high to the upper deck and handed off to another. And there I landed safely, looking down through the railing at the crowd of men and the angry woman.

Suddenly the laughter stopped. The men fell silent and stone still. Then I heard a loud voice behind me shouting down at them. The laughter on their faces died and was replaced by the hard look of their kind. The voice boomed, shattering the air, and the men started returning to their work places. I turned to look up at a tall man with a thick white beard, his arms crossed over a heavy chest, peering down at me with stern eyes. He said nothing and gave nothing, but his eyes locked me in place, and I had more fear of him than even the woman below. But then his eyes released me, and he took a full step forward to the rail. I followed as if it were a command, having to make two steps to equal his one.

The man had come up on deck to join his assistant. Below the bearded man they stood like snow rabbits before the wolf. He thundered at them. They backed off and turned away, but he commanded them forward again. And still he thundered. I looked up at him. His thick white beard was brushed by the wind from the sea. Then he looked down at me, no less severely, but I was certain I saw a slight smile under his whiskers. Then he turned and started away, but realizing I wasn't moving, he turned back and with a wave of his hand made it clear that I was to return to my people. It was no more than a quick wave of his hand, but the meaning was clear. The command absolute. Then his wide figure moved away into the wheelhouse.

When I returned below a crewman was removing the table and chairs. I returned to hugs and laughter. Lisi came to greet me with tears in her eyes. Mother said, "My Maata is a fighter." But I didn't understand that I had done anything. All I had done was run away in fright. The old woman explained later that the boss of the *North Wind* said there will be no more hair cutting unless it is done by him. And if it was done by him, the man with the mustache would be first and his assistant second.

Much later the old woman said to Mother, "My name is Siaja. I will teach the child the language of the Qallunaat. The little I know."

"It is a beginning," my mother said happily.

So that is how the first words of the Qallunaat were taught to me. By an old woman called Siaja over the pounding heart of the *North Wind*.

May 11

I walked a long way out on the sea ice away from Tumak and looked back at the island in its length and remembered what old Siaja had told me. "I will teach you the language of the whites, but you must think in Inuktitut. If you use only their language, you will become as them. And if we lose Inuktitut, we are gone as a people."

"I will remember," I said.

"The first word I will teach you is *Nunavut*. It is a word you must always remember."

"But that is an Inuit word."

"Yes. And you must always remember it the Inuit way. In English it is spoken, 'our land.' Let me hear you say it."

"Nunavut," I said. "Our land."

She was pleased. She nodded, twisting her wrinkled face into a smile. I would learn to speak in English but think always in Inuktitut. For it is our land no matter how many times the Qallunaat say it their way. Long before time. Long before they came, the tundra was our home. "Nunavut," she said.

"Our land," I said. "Nunavut. Land of the Inuit."

Yesterday, at a place where the wind had cleared the snow away, I found old stone tent rings and arrow points and broken caribou bones. It is a place of the ancient ones, where they made camp by the sea long before our time. A hundred winters ago, perhaps more, they put their kayaks into these waters. They hunted here. They were born here and died here. And their bones lay in the earth. A sacred place. Land of the Inuit.

Old Siaja worried she would die on the *North Wind*. She said if she died at sea, they would dump her body into the sea and it would not rest. She had seen this happen on the Yankee whaling ship when she was a young girl. If a sailor died, his body was wrapped and he was slid off into the dark waters.

Siaja believed that her bones should lay in the earth. To sleep on the tundra, with stones to keep the bears away. With stones warmed by the sun in summer and to catch the snow in winter. "Will you promise me this, Maata? You must make this promise to an old woman."

"Yes," I said. And she made the promise between us by taking my small hand tightly in her own. But I was a child, and the promise worried me. Each morning when I woke I would look first to Siaja to see if she was breathing. I would watch for the rise and fall of her old breast under the blanket. And often I would sit and wait until her eyes opened. When she woke she would smile and shake her head. Not this day but soon. Soon, I know.

My lessons began from almost the time Siaja opened her eyes. She started with a few simple words of English, then worked those words into a sentence. And she worked these into my mind by repeating them again and again. I had no knowledge that these words could be put on paper, only that they could be spoken. Writing was something the old woman did not know and I would learn of later. But I found nothing difficult in the language as it was spoken. I learned quickly and I learned much in those few weeks, and Siaja was pleased and so was my mother.

Several times we all gathered up on deck. My father was there with the other men. I went running to him when I saw him, and he swung me up into the air. Swinging me high and out in a big circle, then squeezing me in his arms. "My Maata!" he cried. When he lowered me to see Mother moving out of the crowd of women, he looked hard for a long moment. She came slowly forward with worry in her eyes. Her head was slightly lowered, with just a stubble of hair growing there. Father went to meet her and placed his arm tight about the shoulders. "Am I still your woman?" I heard her ask.

"If you will still have me," he replied. And he added, "You know I am a poor hunter."

"You are a great hunter," she said. "And a better man."

I saw Tiitaa near the railing and went to him,

but for a long moment he ignored me. I tugged at his sleeve, and he finally looked down at me. "Little sister," he said, and that was all he said. There was a large blue mark under his eye and his lip was swollen from where they had thrown him in the boat. He leaned on the rail again, looking far out over the sea. I wanted him to pay attention to me, but he seemed far away.

"Tiitaa?" I said, but his mind was distant. Then I said, "I can talk Qallunaat words. Would you like to hear me?"

After a second he leaned away from the railing and looked down at me. "What?" he asked.

"I can talk like the Qallunaat," I told him proudly.

"But you are an Inuit girl," he said, his voice sharp with anger. And he turned full toward me.

"I know," I told him.

"My sister should not talk the language of the whites," he shouted at me. "Inuktitut is our language! Have you forgotten in only a few days?"

"No," I defended. But he swung away from me and stormed off. I could feel the tears starting to run down my cheeks. I went off to find Mother but couldn't find her, so I ran down the iron stairs to our sleeping place. There Siaja held me to her old body, and I cried heavily. Tiitaa had never before been angry with me.

"It is not you," Siaja explained softly. "The boy is not angry at you."

"But he shouted at me," I managed through the tears.

"He shouted at the Qallunaat," she said. "That was in him before you spoke to him." And she said that Mother was right. I must learn the new language. No matter how angry Tiitaa became.

But even Siaja's words and warm embrace couldn't console me.

Later, when I told my mother of Tiitaa's anger, she didn't seem surprised. She said it would pass away. But the Qallunaat would not. That I must take the words Siaja gave me. And she made me repeat all the new words, even though she couldn't understand them. When I was finished she was pleased and turned to thank Siaja.

"The child has a gift for words," the old woman said. "I think I will try to live long enough to teach her all I know. I only wish I could teach her much more."

"It is a beginning," my mother reminded her.

And old Siaja did live. She did not die on the *North Wind*. Each morning when I woke I watched the rise and fall of her chest and waited for her eyes to open. And on that day when Foster's Bay was sighted, I raced down the iron stairs from the deck and threw myself in her arms. And Mother said to her, "You will come with us. That would make us happy."

"And you will bury me on the tundra?"

"It is a promise."

chapter three

There was a Hudson's Bay Company store and a small school all located near the rocky shore. Beyond these were little houses of wood scattered back to low hills. The houses were very small, like little boxes, and placed in no set order. They were simply here and there. And narrow pipes came up through the roofs, and from a few of them poured a thin gray smoke. The ground was soft and muddy, and patches of snow still lay in the shadow of the hills even in July. Father said we had come farther north. Farther than he had ever been.

It was not what I expected. But it was the total of Foster's Bay. A place built by the Qallunaat, not for them, but for us.

"We will starve here," Tiitaa said on first sight. "There are too many people in one place. We will not find enough caribou. We will empty the sea of seals and fish."

"The government will feed us," said Mother.

But Siaja said, "I fear Tiitaa is right."

First sight was from the rail of the *North Wind* as we were being loaded into the small boats for the short trip over the rough waters of the bay. The sailors were not so impatient with us now. And with us they were loading supplies into the small boats for the Hudson's Bay Company store. As we were lowered to the water, I looked up one last time at the *North Wind,* hoping I would never again walk her deck. I could still hear the pounding of her heart in her iron body. And up at the rail I saw the captain of the sailors. He gazed down at me for an instant, and I know there was a smile under his thick white beard. He gave a slight nod of his head. I gave back a smile, remembering that he had been good to me, and then our boat hit the water and we were moving with the waves to the beach. We were a fleet of small boats loaded with supplies, Inuit, and dogs, lifting and falling on the dark Arctic sea. Mother rested her hand on my shoulder as the settlement appeared above the water and dropped away again. I remember her face still, devoid of expression, her eyes just fixed on the distance.

We were piled out on the shore. Almost immediately the hunters were put to work unloading the supplies from the boats and hauling them up to the Bay store. And as soon as the boats were empty, they went back for another load. When the boats moved off none of us on the beach were sure what to do. Some of the hunters went searching for their dogs. But the dogs, after several weeks at sea and with no whip to control them, were almost impossible to handle. Father returned with only three of the eight that made his team. He looked completely discouraged, but then another hunter brought over two more, knowing they belonged to my father.

For a long time all the people stayed gathered near the shore, milling about aimlessly. One would ask another what they should do, where they should go next. But always the others would shake their heads and shrug their shoulders, looking confused. Two more trips were made with the small boats back to the *North Wind* before the ship was empty of Inuit and all were on shore. Then the small boats left for the last time with no word to us from the sailors. And a short time after that, after the boats were pulled up to hang at her sides, the *North Wind* moved slowly out of the bay and up on the horizon, becoming smaller and smaller with a line of smoke running from her stack. A little toy boat disappearing over the curve of the earth.

Evening started to fall, and still we were all gathered there. Hekenjuk moving low over the tundra. But Father said there would be little darkness because we were so far north now. Children started to complain of hunger, and infants were taken to their mothers' breasts. A few of the hunters found driftwood to build fires and those who had dried meat or fish shared it. There was not much, but we all shared. And Tiitaa complained angrily that this was the beginning of starvation. The way the Qallunaat would feed us.

I looked to my mother with fear in my eyes, for even with my eight winters I knew that starvation could be a horrible reality on the tundra. It was not a word to be spoken lightly. Mother took Tiitaa a short distance from us, and I could just hear her harsh words echo back. When they returned Tiitaa's head was low and his look brooding.

We were a long time on the rocky beach, huddled near the fires as a cold wind moved off the ocean. Then a hunter stood up and walked down near the water. Several others joined him, and they stood listening. What they heard, though none of us knew then, was the sound of an engine in a small boat. Soon we could all hear the steady hum of it, though none could see it. Then it came from beyond a point of land, skipping over the surface of the sea. It was bigger than a kayak but not as big as the boats carried on the *North Wind*. It was a Peterhead boat, with a single mast for a sail and with an inboard engine. And though it was a strange sight for us gathered that evening, it would in a short time become a regular tool for the hunters who settled Foster's Bay and a common sight on all the waters of the north. My father and the others watched in wonder as it came toward the shore. Then the noise of it died away, and it coasted over the waves to the rocky beach. Two Qallunaat climbed out, and the hunters helped them haul the boat partway up the beach. The two men stood for a moment looking at us curiously. Then one of them stepped forward and spoke in almost perfect Inuktitut. "My name is Daniel Morgan," he said. "This is my friend John Olson. Why are you people gathered here?"

The people were all so taken by this man's clear use of their language that for a moment none replied. Then Father spoke for all of them. "We were brought by the *North Wind*. They put us here in this place."

The man, Morgan, looked at his friend. They both looked out at the empty sea. Then they looked at each other.

Father continued. "The government said we must come to this place. They said they would feed us." He waited. The men said nothing in return. As if not certain what to say next, Father said, "I have lost three dogs from my team. And I will need to build a new *kamotik* before the snows come." Again he was quiet. Then he asked, "Are you the government?"

Morgan replied, "No. I have nothing to do with the government here."

"Then where should we find the government?"

Morgan shook his head. He turned suddenly and moved through the crowd, with the people making way for him. Olson followed. They walked down the beach, then up to one of the small wood huts. Morgan pounded on the door of the hut. They waited a moment, and when there was nothing Morgan pounded again. Still there was nothing. Morgan stepped aside, and Olson came up to the door with the full weight of his boot. The door sprang open, with the whole hut shaking. We all watched in amazement as Olson went in and came out dragging a man by the collar. The man had a bottle in his hand, and when Olson freed him he fell to the ground. Morgan picked up the bottle and swung it far out to sea. The man tried to get up on his feet, but then he fell again. Olson went into the hut, and when he came out there was a crate on his shoulder filled with bottles. One by one he started smashing them on the rocks. We could all hear the man on the ground protesting loudly. When Olson was finished with the bottles, he lifted the man by the back of his belt and hauled him down the beach. Then he lifted him high in the air and threw him into the sea. We all started laughing.

Olson returned to the hut to make another search. Morgan came back to where we were waiting. He frightened me a little now, and I moved behind Tiitaa. Morgan's voice rolled loudly: "For this day you all have a new government. I am it. First we will find a house for each family. After you are settled in we will see that you have supplies." He started up from the beach, and the people followed him. I tried to stay with Tiitaa, but Tiitaa was moving much too fast. I looked for Mother and Siaja, but the people had all started to move at once and I couldn't find them. Then I stumbled over the rocks and fell. Two large hands reached under my arms and lifted me to my feet. I turned to see Olson, who had come up behind me. I turned and ran as fast as I could away from him.

I could hear his laughter rolling up behind me, as I scurried over the rocks. When I looked back again Olson had a husky pup under one arm and with his free hand he was helping the women with their bundles.

And that is how we started our life at Foster's Bay.

I saw another large flock of geese this morning, a dark wave close in over the sea ice, but none stopped at Tumak. Soon other birds will follow. I will have eggs from the eider ducks and gulls.

I saw a fox when I was out walking. He was running along the beach, and I could have shot him dead with the rifle. But I have no need for him so I let him run free. I think he is hoping for the geese to return, just as I am. Then he and I will be in competition for the eggs and maybe then I will shoot him.

Across the island there is a narrow slip in the channel that is free of ice. It is not much. I could jump easily across it. But the sea is running smoothly through, and it has not closed for several days. Another good sign that soon the sea ice will break. I could cross it to the open tundra and be off the island. But I worry that the ice would open even more and that I could not return. It is best not to risk it. And, anyway, I have no good reason for doing it.

May 16

The little house in Foster's Bay had a glass window. Father was fascinated by the window. Every so often he would go up and tap his fingers against the glass and smile. Then he would press his nose against it, looking out. We all laughed at him, and he laughed with us.

There was a small iron stove to build a fire. Father made a fire, and the little house filled with smoke so we all had to leave. Mother sent Tiitaa to find Morgan. Tiitaa instead came back with Olson, who showed Father how to open the flue in the pipe that went outside. For a long time after that, Father no longer trusted the stove and Mother built all the fires.

There was no sleeping ledge. Olson explained that in Qallunaat homes there is no such thing as a sleeping ledge. Mother did not like this and said that in time we would build one. Olson said he understood and would later try to help. Mother laid the caribou skins on the floor along the walls for a sleeping place.

We were told that we could get some credit at the Bay Company store. Credit for food and clothes. But when we went to the store, Mother didn't understand the food except for the tea and sugar. And the clothes, she said, would never keep the Inuit warm. So she got tobacco for Father and a big bag of sugar candy for me. Siaja and I sat in our sleeping place and ate the whole bag of candy. Later Morgan told Mother that she should be careful how she used the credit. He said the man at the store should have explained it to her. He took mother and me back to the store, and I could tell from his words that he was quite angry with the man behind the counter. The man said nothing to Morgan but listened solemnly. And after that I got no more candy. And Father did not get tobacco again until he had white fox to trade when the snows came.

Morgan said things would get better at Foster's bay, and they did. Before the first snows fell there was a new government official to replace the old. The Royal Canadian Mounted Police established a post. The government sent a teacher for the little school. Even a nursing station was opened. It all happened so fast. And Foster's Bay was growing from the sea back to the low hills. And Siaja kept saying, "So many people. So very many people."

Morgan explained that the government wanted Foster's Bay to be an example for other Inuit to come off the tundra and into settlements. When my father asked if this was good, Morgan shrugged his shoulders and said, "I don't know. I think there is some good in it. But also some bad. We will know in time. And in time only you can give that answer."

"No," Father said. "In time it will be Tiitaa and Maata who will answer. Not us old ones."

Morgan looked at my father with respect. "There will be changes," he said. "Many changes.

And change is always difficult. You will gain new things. But you must be careful of those things you lose."

Father nodded thoughtfully. "Yes," he said. "This I know."

Morgan was a good friend to my father. He even helped him acquire enough wood to build a fine new *kamotik* before the snows came. And when the wood was gathered both Morgan and Olson helped to build the sled. But the thing that fascinated my father most was Morgan's boat. As the weeks passed by, more and more of these boats appeared along the beach, and my father would go down almost every day to admire them. Then one day Morgan asked him if he would like to take a ride out over the water. Father beamed with excitement. And because I was there, Morgan swung me into the boat beside my father.

Morgan started the engine, and soon we were skipping over the dark water running far out to sea. I could feel the wind on my face and moving through my hair. When I looked at my father he had a large grin on his face, and he looked down at me and nodded. "Fine thing," he said, with deep pleasure. "Truly a fine thing. A man should have a boat such as this. Isn't that true, Maata?"

"Yes," I said.

"Yes," he said, in total agreement. "It is almost a necessary thing." And he went over and leaned close to the cover of the inboard engine. And again he nodded. "It breathes good," he said.

There were a few drifting floes of ice on the sea, and these Morgan worked the boat through. In most places the surface of the water was covered only with slush ice. After a time Morgan made a wide turn, and we were moving straight off the coast away from Foster's Bay. The sound of the engine grew louder as we picked up speed. The force of the wind stronger. Father's joy greater.

We were far out from shore when we saw the bear. Morgan pointed ahead of us and, turning, I saw him climbing up on one of the ice floes. He was a big bear, almost too big for the small floe to support, and the seawater was still rushing off his white body as he turned to look at us. He was a long way off, but we appeared to be moving up on him rapidly. Father moved close beside me. "Look, Maata!"

"Yes. I see him," I said.

"He is a fine bear," said Father, and I could hear the delight of the whole thing filling his voice. My father was having one of the very best times of his life.

The bear plunged off the floe and when he surfaced again swam for a short time just in front of the boat. We could see his head and powerful neck above the water and the white length of his body below it. Then Morgan slowed the engine and turned away. We watched as the bear climbed up on another floe. Then the engine grew louder and the boat made a half circle, turning back toward Foster's Bay.

Then Morgan looked at my father and asked, "Would you like to take the tiller?"

For a moment my father looked paralyzed. Then he nodded, as if coming out of a trance.

Morgan slowed the boat so it was just moving easily over the water. Then he took Father's hand and placed it on the tiller. He rested his hand over the hunter's. Father was no longer grinning. At first there was a strange seriousness on his face, then slowly, so very slowly, he started to smile. "Look, Maata!" he said.

"I see, Father."

He was driving the boat.

Morgan laughed and I laughed, but my father was still too serious to laugh, though he held the smile. And at that moment I was very proud of my father. And at that moment I loved Daniel Morgan more than any man in the world.

With Morgan's help Father ran the boat almost back to Foster's Bay. And then it was my turn. Morgan let me take the tiller, resting his strong hand on mine.

Father nodded his head. "It is a fine thing," he said once again. "Almost a necessary thing."

May 19

For two days the sun has been warm and bright on Tumak. Hekenjuk smiles boldly while Taktik spends more time at home. The snow melts slowly, and small streams flow between the rocks. Today I walked far to the end of the island to find a place where the geese are nesting, but I found nothing. I found fox tracks. Maybe the same old fox searching as I was searching.

At a place where the rocks were warm from the sun and water flowed from under the melting snow, I stopped to rest. There I used Morgan's coat for a blanket and took off all my things to wash my body in the melting snow, just as my mother washed me as a child. The snow was cold and bit my flesh as it melted in my hands. The water in the small stream swirled about my feet. Then I lay back to feel the warmth of Hekenjuk, and I watched for a time the clouds drifting above me and could feel the earth move under me. The earth carrying my body through time, so free that the motion almost made me dizzy. I closed my eyes to ride the quiet, but the light of the sun filtered into my mind. Then the wind came up from the sea ice to chill my body. And I pulled the coat tight, crossing the arms over me. And for a long time I lay that way, feeling the motion of the earth, the chill of the wind, and the warmth of the sun. So free.

When I returned to the cabin Morgan looked worried. "You've been gone all day," he said.

I told him I went looking for the geese. But I found none on Tumak.

He said no more and I was quiet. But later he asked if the small channel was still free of ice.

I told him I did not go that way. "But I saw a cloud low over the sea ice. I think there may be open water."

"Yes," he said. "That is a sign." But I knew by his voice he had doubt. Then he was quiet.

✳

May 20

In the early winter of 1914 I attended school for the first time. The school in Foster's Bay was one small room heated by an iron stove. Long benches ran across the room, and a narrow table ran the length of each bench. There were only about ten students, some a little older and some younger than myself.

In the beginning we had no books, only pencils and paper, and the teacher wrote our lessons on a large chalkboard. The iron stove was in the front, near the teacher's desk, but still he appeared always to be cold. He walked back and forth in front of the board, rubbing his hands, and he always kept his coat on. Those first winter weeks he covered the walls with old newspapers to keep the drafts out. He was thin as a rail, with a narrow face and a sharp nose. When he was pacing his head was lowered and a wisp of gray hair hung down over his eyes. He was very serious, seldom laughed. Whenever he looked up at us, we all quickly lowered our heads to our papers. His name was Sanders. That was the first word he taught us to write in English and the first word he taught us to say as a class.

All of our lessons were in English from the very first day. We learned later that Mr. Sanders could speak Inuktitut, though he spoke it poorly. But he never spoke our native language in class. Thanks to Siaja, I was more advanced than the others, and I soon became the teacher's favorite. I liked school. In truth, I loved learning, and language came easily to me. In the evenings I had Siaja to help me and Mother to encourage me.

But Tiitaa was very annoyed that no respect was given to our native language. He was even more annoyed when I told him even the songs we sang here were in English. And when I tried to sing one of them for him, Father roared with laughter. "What a terrible thing," Father said. And when I tried to translate the words of the song into Inuktitut, my father laughed even harder. "The Qallunaat have no knowledge of song words," he said. And he took the same words and sang them in his hunter's voice adding, "Ayaa-yaa. Ayaa-yaa." Siaja joined in, clapping her hands with a big smile wrinkling her face and her eyes twinkling. Mother laughed and I laughed. But Tiitaa was solemn. And before the singing was finished he left the house and went off into the darkness. When he was gone and the laughter had stopped, I heard Mother whisper, "We will lose him."

Looking at her, my father nodded slowly.

I loved Tiitaa, and I worried about him that first winter in Foster's Bay. For Tiitaa had changed. He no longer spoke to me and laughed with me as he once had. He no longer played games and teased me. I badly missed his attention, and there were times when I believed he didn't love me.

At the end of the first month of school, Mr. Sanders set a large box on his desk and one at a time called us to the front of the room. As each of us came forward, he handed us a book. It was a very quiet ceremony, with Mr. Sanders in his sober manner eyeing our reactions carefully. When it came my time and he laid the small book in my hand, almost like a sacred thing, he gave the slightest nod of his head. When all the books were handed out and we had returned to our places, he said, "I have given you the world. It is in your hands. Never again can you say to others that you never had a chance in life."

I treasured my small book. My first book. It was all in English. Not an Inuktitut word in it. Even the pictures were of Qallunaat children. I remember running all the way back home in the deep snow to share my book with Siaja and how she and I huddled for hours going over the pages, the words and the pictures. I was already surpassing Siaja's knowledge of English, and she was pleased that now I could take words from paper.

I studied for long hours each evening in the dim light of the lamp. In no time I had gone through the first few chapters. I learned them so well, I could almost recite them. And I would go on far ahead of the classwork to discover new words. Each new word was like a gift. And when that word joined with others, it was like a miracle. They painted pictures in my mind, and my mind ran with them.

At times Mr. Sanders would call on me to read for the class. And when others had trouble with their studies, he would ask me to work with them for a time in the far back of the room. I didn't realize how this set me apart from others. I never thought about it. Not until our first real spelling test came and I was the only one in class to come away with a small gold star on my paper. All eyes in the room locked on me as Mr. Sanders said, "If the rest of you took the time, only half the time, to study as Maata does, the class would be through this book and well into the next one."

I sat with my head lowered, but still I could feel the glare of the class.

We were well into winter darkness then. Taktik came early, and I walked home through the settlement under his light. But I hadn't gone far that evening when several boys approached me.

"The Qallunaaq gave Maata a star," one laughed. And another demanded, "Let us see the star, Maata."

A boy stepped forward and tried to pull the book and papers from my arms, but I fought back. Then another pushed me down into the snow and held me there, pressing his hands down on my arms. A boy opened my precious book and pretended to read, mocking me in the way I read before the class, and they all started laughing. Then he threw the book high into the air under the light of Taktik. I remember watching the book going up and the pages opening. As it fell another boy caught it, and they let me up out of the snow. Soon I was running from boy to boy, trying hopelessly to catch my book, for I could not reach their height or jump as high. Their laughter was cruel, and I was too angry for tears.

Then the book went up again, so far up, and came almost floating down. A hand reached out and took it easily, and the laughter ended quickly. Catching the book in one hand, Tiitaa stepped forward and with one blow sent the largest boy rolling into the snow. Then, turning to the second largest, he did the same. He turned to the others, but they were on the run. Then Tiitaa turned to me and said, "Go home, Maata." He returned my book and I collected my papers. When the first boy got up Tiitaa hit him hard.

I could hear the loud *smack!* Then Tiitaa turned to me again and said, "Go home, Maata." It was a direct order.

"No," I said. "I want to watch."

Tiitaa hesitated, then nodded. He picked up the second boy who raised his hand to defend himself, but not quickly enough. *Smack!* And, *smack! Smack! Smack!* The boy went down.

The first started to crawl away. I stepped on his back to slow him. Tiitaa lifted him by the hair. *Smack! Smack!* "You will remember me," Tiitaa told them. "You will remember me each time you look at my sister." *Smack!*

We walked home through the settlement, Tiitaa and I, walking by the light Taktik laid on the snow. Past the yellow window lights and the sleeping dogs. With the smell of smoke from the narrow chimney pipes. I had to walk a little faster to keep pace with Tiitaa, but I kept pace. And not a word was spoken. Not a word was needed.

May 22

There was a shaman in Foster's Bay that first dark winter. He was called Pavvik. He was not of our band. We hardly knew him. He was of others who came on the boat as we did. But we were no longer separated as a group. We were all part of the settlement. As he was respected by those who knew him, he also came to be respected by us. Kuliaq, the hunter who was the husband of Lisi, my mother's sister, came to know this shaman well. The two became close friends and that autumn hunted caribou and in the winter trapped white fox. The white fox pelts were used for trade at the Hudson's Bay Company store. The fur of the white fox helped to supplement the small family allowances given to us by the government. All the hunters went to take some caribou and white fox. And they took some seal. And on occasion a hunter might bring in a snow bear. These all helped to build credit at the Bay store.

It was Lisi who asked Kuliaq to bring this

shaman to Siaja when Siaja fell ill. Siaja would not go to the nursing station run by the government. She lay on her sleeping place, fighting for each breath. Pavvik started by simply listening to her. He stood for a long time just listening. Then, from his bag, he took a *memeo*, a thin oval blade of wood tied to a long cord. Slowly he started to whirl this in the air, slowly in the beginning, and then faster and faster until the sound of it filled the room. As the *memeo* wailed, Pavvik began a chant. At first I could hardly hear his words, but then the chant grew louder and louder. As the shadow of the *memeo* passed over Siaja's old body, Pavvik's words kept pace with it. Then, suddenly, Pavvik stopped. He fell quiet and carefully returned the *memeo* to his bag.

What Pavvik did next frightened me. He took his right hand and laid it over Siaja's nose and mouth. And he held it there so long that I was sure she couldn't breathe. Siaja was gasping for air when finally Pavvik removed his right hand and cupped it into his left. Then, without a word, he went outside. Mother, Tiitaa, and I followed him. We followed him in a full circle around the little house. He walked with his hands tight together, breaking a path in the deep snow. And as he walked, he started to sing. He sang a spirit song. And he sang in that language that only shamans know. Then he opened his hands to the wind. Then he turned to us and nodded. And then he walked away. He went home.

When we went back to Siaja she was sleeping easily, and her breathing was no longer labored. I watched the rise and fall of her chest to be certain she was alive. Mother said, "Pavvik took the badness from her body. He gave it to the wind to carry to the far side of the earth."

"She is not going to die?" I asked Mother.

"She is old," Mother said. "This time death passed her by. But he will be back. And not even Pavvik will stop him when the time comes."

So for many mornings after, as I had on the ship, when I opened my eyes I went to old Siaja to be certain she was breathing. And most often she would wake with a smile and take me in her arms. "Not now, Maata. Not now." And I would huddle in close to her.

Pavvik was respected. There were other, lesser shamans in Foster's Bay. But none with his reputation. It was even said that Pavvik, in a trance, had once flown to the moon. That he has visited with Taktik and looked down upon the sea of ice and endless tundra. And that another time, in his youth, he had taken the form of a snow bear for an entire winter. I believed these things. In truth, I don't doubt them now. For the Inuit know such things happen. Even if the Qallunaat do not.

But that winter in Foster's Bay an evil spirit took hold of Pavvik. A spirit with more power than any he had ever known. Pavvik discovered a drink the Qallunaat call *whiskey*. He believed this gave him great visions. That it placed him above fear and made his mind work in ways that it had never worked before. And once on a hunt Pavvik shared this drink with Kuliaq. And through it they believed they shared the same vision. I heard Kuliaq speak of this to my father. How they could pass their hands through fire and not feel the pain. How they could walk in bare feet through the snow and not feel the cold. "It is true," Kuliaq swore. "And Pavvik believes it is the whiskey that makes the Qallunaat know so many things we do not know."

When Morgan came to visit, Father asked him about this, and Morgan replied, "It is one of the changes we talked about. One the Inuit must face. But a bad one. It will make them sick. It will destroy them."

My father warned Kuliaq of this. But Kuliaq
went on following Pavvik. No one knew where
they got the whiskey, though it was believed from
the man who ran the Bay Company store. It was
believed the whiskey was bought with the fur of
the white fox.

Lisi was a good woman. She had not given
Kuliaq any children yet, but they had lived together
only a short time. And Kuliaq was a good hunter,
and it was certain to all that he loved Lisi dearly.
When Kuliaq returned from a long hunt, one
could see the joy in Lisi's eyes. But in the darkness
of that winter, all that started to change. And my
mother was the first to realize the change. She saw
it in her sister. Lisi would come to visit us more
often and stay much longer. There were some
nights when she didn't return home at all. I
remember one night when Kuliaq came looking
for her, pounding on the door of our small house
and waking us. Father went out to talk to him, and
after a time Kuliaq went away. But Lisi sat in the
corner all night without sleeping. And the next
day, when she did return to Kuliaq, both Mother
and Father went along with her.

At times Lisi would come to visit and fall into a
long silence, talking only now and then to Mother.

In the past she would listen as I read pages from my book, and she would praise me. But now she had fallen quiet. Often there would be bruises on her face or arms, and she would sit in the shadows shamefully. But I knew Lisi had done nothing to be ashamed of. She was always Lisi.

Tiitaa said it was the whiskey. And he said it bitterly. Father sadly agreed. Morgan was right. It made them sick. And Kuliaq did nothing but drink the whiskey.

"He is not a hunter now. And he does not care for his woman," Mother said.

There was talk of Pavvik in the settlement. The people had lost respect for him. They no longer asked his advice or went to him for spirit songs. They said he had not the strength even to help himself.

All of this was happening over the long weeks of winter. A few words spoken. Some tears. Kuliaq pounding on our door in anger. At other times pleading and weeping. Kuliaq promising and Lisi returning. It filled our little house with an uneasiness that was always on Mother's face, that invaded our lives, for my mother worried greatly for her sister.

I went off to school one morning, and as I neared Lisi's little house I saw people gathered there. They were standing silently in the cold. Saying nothing, waiting. Then two men came out of the house and down the steps. They were the Royal Canadian Mounted Police stationed at Foster's Bay, and between them was Kuliaq. They had Kuliaq by the arms and he was weeping. I have never seen a man weep in such a way. As they were leading him off, I heard a voice in the crowd say, "She was a good woman. All she did, she did for him." And hearing it, a chill ran through my body. "Lisi?" I asked.

A woman came toward me and said, "Go get Nua, Maata. Run home and get your mother."

I turned and ran for home, running over the same snow path I took for school, passing Lisi's little house each morning. But as I neared our house Mother was coming toward me. She had been told. Word had reached her. "Go back home," she said. "And wait for me there."

"But I want to see Lisi."

"Go home," she told me. "Go and stay with Siaja." Her voice was absolute, and I didn't argue. She was very firm and in complete control. The way she was with all things. I watched her going down the path, and as she neared Lisi's door the crowd made way for her. I waited on the path in the cold darkness of that morning. Just waiting for her to return. Something inside me refused to move until Mother returned and took my hand. And I thought about Lisi. Lisi, when they cut her hair away during our passage on the *North Wind*. Lisi, who listened quietly as I read words from my book. And how her eyes filled with joy when Kuliaq returned from a hunt.

Lisi's grave was the first in Foster's Bay. High up on a hill. They could not dig deep because the earth was frozen. But the men gathered many large rocks. Mother and I stood watching as they placed the rocks, Mother making certain each was carefully placed, and then we stood a long time after all the others had gone away.

The RCMP took Kuliaq away by dog team. They said there would be trial under Qallunaat law. They said it was almost certain he would spend many years in jail. It was said later that he died in prison. That his soul died. For to lock up any Inuit is to kill him slowly but surely.

"Kuliaq crushed her head with the club he used to kill seals," my father told Morgan.

Morgan said it was the whiskey.

Father told Morgan he had warned them about the whiskey.

Morgan shook his head regretfully. He asked what had become of Pavvik.

Father shrugged his shoulders. "None have seen him since they took Kuliaq away."

Some in the settlement said Pavvik went off alone over the ice. A few of his dogs came back lean and hungry. And he had been drinking the whiskey.

"A bad thing," Morgan said.

And Father agreed. A bad thing. And a sad thing for us. "But who knows?" Father added thoughtfully. "Perhaps it is that Pavvik decided to turn again into a snow bear and is spending the winter on the sea ice."

"Perhaps," said Morgan.

"Yes. Perhaps. And that would be a better thing," said my father. "A fine thing."

chapter four

I was ten years of age when Tiitaa left us. Tiitaa
had grown to be a man and had a reputation as
one of the best hunters in Foster's Bay. He had
made several trips north with Morgan and Olson.
Morgan hired Tiitaa to take care of the dogs and
bring in game. On these trips Tiitaa always saw
new country. New places. And his heart seldom
returned with him. No sooner would he return
than he was restless to leave again. The settlement
for Tiitaa was a place where his *ino*, his life-soul,
would never be content.

On one trip Tiitaa made with Morgan and Olson, he was gone all winter. They left Foster's Bay as soon as the autumn snow started to fall and did not return until spring. They traveled north for those first weeks, running their teams while Hekenjuk was still long in the sky. Far north of the Arctic Circle they came to a place called Igloolik. In our language Igloolik means "a place of houses." It was a settlement just as Foster's Bay is a settlement. But Tiitaa said later that there were not as many houses as in Foster's Bay. "It was a little place," he said. "Few people. And the last government place."

After they had rested their teams at Igloolik, they crossed Fox Basin over the sea ice and traveled to the north of Baffin Island. They were traveling into the arms of winter, and it was coming fast upon them. Morgan and Olson were ready to turn back and spend the dark months at Igloolik when they came upon a small camp. A group of snow houses near the place the Qallunaat now call Arctic Bay. There a small band of Inuit who still followed the old ways, true Inutuinnait, had made a winter camp. They came upon this place just as the wind from the north covered the land with a blinding snow. And there they were welcomed by the people.

They wintered there. And there Tiitaa took to his sleeping place a girl called Inuppak. A girl of great beauty with hair the color of a raven's wings. And she became Tiitaa's woman.

There was great joy in our house when Tiitaa returned in the spring. Bundled on his sled was the beautiful Inuppak. She was so bright and cheerful, she was like a gift sent by Hekenjuk. Mother welcomed her with open arms. Siaja fussed over her. Father offered her the greatest respect, and I followed her about like a puppy. She quickly became my older sister and treated me in just that way.

I filled Inuppak's time those first few days showing her about the settlement. And showing her off. "This is Tiitaa's woman," I would say proudly, and step out of the viewer's sight. "She comes from the north country. Her name is Inuppak." And then I would watch as they admired her. And all admired her, even those who said little. The hunters who gathered at the Bay Company store fell silent. Even my teacher, Mr. Sanders, lifted his head high and pushed the hair back from his face. When I walked through the settlement with Inuppak, I walked a little prouder. And I tried to fashion myself after her.

Her movements. Her smile. The softness of her voice. Her shyness.

Once Mother whispered to me, "Now I have two beautiful daughters. How can a woman be so lucky?" And I could hear the happiness in her voice. And I was as happy as Mother.

My happiness ended when I heard Tiitaa tell Father they would be leaving. Returning to Inuppak's people.

"Her people are free," Tiitaa said. "They still follow the seasons. They are not fixed like the people here. And I must be free."

Our father showed no emotions. He simply rested his hand on Tiitaa's shoulder and nodded his understanding. It was as he knew it would be.

And it appeared Mother understood as well, for all she did was take Tiitaa and then Inuppak in her arms and hold them tight. Rocking them against her body as if she would hold them that way through eternity. In a mother's way.

But I did not understand. And I did not accept. And I bit my lip in silence. I did not want to lose Tiitaa. And in my thoughts I believe Inuppak would now be with us always. That our family had grown stronger and more enjoyable. That we were a whole and that Inuppak had added strength to the whole. It was Siaja who first noticed how unhappy I was.

"Nothing has changed," Siaja told me. "Tiitaa has been gone all winter, and now he is going away again. Tiitaa still loves you, and now you have Inuppak who loves you also. People often scatter the way the wind scatters the falling snow. But you still love them and they love you."

Siaja's words were spoken with deep feelings, but they did not help me. And after a time I found myself blaming Inuppak for everything. I became bitter toward Inuppak. I seldom spoke to her, and I outwardly avoided her. I thought that Inuppak should realize my unhappiness. But strangely, she hardly seemed to notice, and this hurt even more. As if I didn't matter. Then one evening Inuppak did something to change my feelings completely. It was only a few words spoken. But it was so unexpected, and it came from her heart. She asked Mother in her quiet way, "When Tiitaa and I return north it would make me happy if Maata could go with us." I had become as a sister to her, she told my mother. And she and Tiitaa would take the very best care of me.

I sat up listening, and for the first time in days there was a smile on my face. Siaja looked at me and offered a wink of her eye. My mother was thoughtful. She saw my happiness, started to speak, then hesitated. But after a moment she said, "Maata must stay here and stay in school. The Qallunaaq who is her teacher said she has a gift of words. She must continue to learn."

I was a little sad but not completely disappointed. For I loved school, and I also wanted to continue. But at the same time I would have liked to travel north with Tiitaa and Inuppak.

Mother continued, saying to Inuppak, "Your people move like the wind. Our people, Krakoluk's band and others, are fixed here in Foster's Bay. I know that in time your people will also be forced to live as we do. For now the things that Maata will need to know in her life she can learn only here. Later, when that is done, she can join you and Tiitaa if that is her wish." Mother's words were final but not spoken harshly.

And later, when Tiitaa posed the same question to our father, Father simply shook his head. "Nua has spoken," he said. "She sees things with Maata in a different way. I may not agree always, but Nua is a strong woman in her mind. And oftentimes she has been right. I know she will be right with Maata."

And so it was decided that I would remain in

Foster's Bay. But I moved closer to my sister Inuppak. And it became as though our blood were the same.

May 26

Last night in the thin hours of darkness, I heard the ice break far out on the bay. It came with a loud rolling boom. Like thunder. The pressure of the ice building, with one large block pushed up on another. I woke from my sleeping place and ran outside. Under the narrow light of Taktik, below a black heaven of stars, the moaning and the cracking continued. The sea in agony. The locked land tearing free. I turned to wake Morgan but found him behind me, leaning his weight in the doorway, looking off in the distance. Neither of us spoke but stood together listening. He took my hand and squeezed it tightly. I rested my head against his shoulder. There were tears in my eyes, but they were good tears. The clearing of the ice has started early. Just as the geese flew early above us.

I think soon the bay will be free. And we will see the black smoke from a ship on the horizon.

When dawn came there were new ice ridges in the distance. Pressure ice formed by one floe being pressed against another. I could see them in the field glasses.

Late in the morning I slung the rifle over my shoulder and went down to the sea ice. I walked a long way out from Tumak. Over the dark sea, over the still-frozen ice. But I could see fractures and in a few places even narrow leads opening up. I did not go beyond what I thought was safe for fear that the ice would open under me. And I could still hear the booming off in the distance. And at times I could even feel the ice alive under me, quivering like an animal in pain. Then in the field glasses I could clearly see the large blocks shifting and thrusting up, one on another. Some as large as small islands and as thick as I am tall.

There will be no more talk of my walking out alone, of my crossing the sea ice to Seal Bay. There is no leaving Tumak now until the ship comes. The *North Wind* or the *Venture*. I was never sure I could make it alone, not on foot. And if I were lost on the ice, there would be no one for Morgan.

May 28

My birth date. Morgan said nothing to me about my birth date. On this day I have seventeen years.

And I said nothing to Morgan about it either. I thought I would let the day go away like yesterday, and tomorrow.

I went up to Olson's grave and sat there for a time. I fixed the stones in place and thought about my friend Olson. I could still hear the ice shifting and breaking far out on the bay. But below the sound of the ice, there was only the soft voice of the wind.

I remember another birth date. Back in Foster's Bay. When Siaja gave me an amulet. Olson gave me a wordbook. I treasured both greatly. The amulet I wear about my neck. A small snowbird carved from the ivory of a walrus. It is very old and yellowed and polished from age. Siaja said it had been given to her when she was a girl by an old woman who was older than time. And it was given to the old woman by a shaman who carved the ivory.

"In it there is power," Siaja said. "Not great power. But a little is better than none."

I worried when Siaja's shaking hands laid the gift in mine. I told her she should not part with it.

She closed my fingers around the small ivory carving and held them tight for a moment. She said she had no use for such things any longer. "I am tired and ready to accept sleep. And I am happy because you have filled my life these last years. Please allow me the joy of giving this gift."

I promised to wear it until I was an old woman. And then pass it on to another.

Siaja nodded her head. Her eyes bright with happiness. "And tell that person Siaja gave it to you. Siaja, who taught you your first English words. The old woman whose breathing you listened for each morning. Tell them, and I will be remembered," she said.

I promised she would always be remembered. And her name passed on.

Siaja would listen as I read from the wordbook Olson gave me. It was a big, heavy book. So heavy I had to rest it across my legs as I sat on the sleeping place. It was new, and the pages had that sweet, clean smell, as only new books have. And in it a man named Webster put all the words he knew in English. I could find any word I wanted and even words I had never known before.

I called it my wintertime book. And I told Siaja I would read all of it before Hekenjuk returned in the spring.

Siaja thought it was far too much.

"No," I said. And I started reading from the

first word on the very first page of words. "'The letter *A*,'" I said. "'The first letter of the English alphabet. From the Greek *alpha*. A borrowing from the Phoenicians.'"

"Who are the Phoenicians?" asked Siaja.

I told her I didn't know. But I was certain if I read on, I would learn about them.

"They must live beyond the sea ice," said Siaja. And she said it is not good to borrow. It is better to trade. Or to have something given to you freely. Then, after a moment, she asked most seriously, "Could I hold the book in my hands?"

I shifted the weight of the book over to her, and she held it, resting it on her lap, thoughtfully. She let her trembling fingers run through the pages. "Such a wonderful book," she said. "All of these words. More words than flakes of snow. But what will you do with all of these words, Maata?"

"I don't know," I said honestly. "But when I learn a word I find that it belongs to another word. And they belong to others. And I can write on paper all the things I think. And what I have seen I can give to others." And holding the amulet in my hand, I told her it was just as the amulet was given to me through her. A snowbird carved from ivory but before that in the mind of the carver long ago.

Siaja nodded her old head. She smiled with tired eyes. She told me my mother was right. The things I must learn now are in Foster's Bay. I could not learn them up north with Tiitaa and Inuppak. Then she pushed the book back to me, and I took the weight from her carefully. "On this birth date you were given two amulets," she told me. "But perhaps the one Olson gave you has more power than mine."

I moved the book to one side, then laid my head to rest in Siaja's lap. Her fingers combed lovingly through my long black hair. "My little Maata," she whispered. "Child of the snow. Daughter of the wind. I think you will always move between the world of the Inuit and the world of the Qallunaat. I think it is to be that way. Just as Nua has known it would be. Just as she knew Tiitaa could live only in the world of his ancestors."

May 29

The sea ice still thunders and moans. The ice ridges change and shift. They vanish and reappear again. Always moving in closer to Tumak. It may take days. Even weeks. But the clearing has started. A wide channel is forming through the ice, cutting in toward the island. I saw several bears hunting near the open water, looking for seals. When all the ice is gone the bears will gather on the land, foraging for what food they can find. They will lose their white and turn a dirty yellow through the summer. And they will become lean and irritable. They will feed on carrion or berries. They will come in close to the cabin if there is the smell of meat. They will be troublesome and most dangerous.

I thought about my father today and his boat and the big bear he killed that first winter when Tiitaa had gone north again.

Father had set it in his mind that he would have one of the Peterhead boats he so admired. One of the fine boats that would take him far out over the open sea. And Father learned that the man who ran the Bay Company store had such a boat to offer. The boat had belonged to an Inuit who borrowed much from the store and couldn't pay it back. So the boat had been taken in payment. And now the Bay Company man offered the boat in trade. So as soon as the first snows started to fall, as soon as the cold winds came, my father set his traps for the white fox. His intention was to collect enough white fox through the winter to own the boat in spring. Enough furs to trade evenly. And often he would be gone for days at a time, far off from the settlement, to find the best place for his traps. He worked very hard through those dark months. And Mother and I worked with him, stretching and cleaning the hides he brought back. Slowly but surely, Father built his credit, with a smile on his face each time he brought in his furs and the man marked them in the book. By the time half the dark winter had passed, my father had half of his payment for the boat. But then a series of bad storms hit Foster's Bay. Blizzards that came in one after another, with terrible winds and heavy snows. Not one hunter ventured out of the settlement. To do so could easily mean death. It was so bitter cold that even my going the short distance to the school was dangerous. Mr. Sanders kept the iron stove at the front of the room cherry red. And we could hear the wind whistle through the walls.

The settlement was locked in under the storms. The little houses covered to their roofs with snow and the snow frozen solid on the surface. The storms lasted days, and the days turned to more days. Just as one would blow through, another would follow. And Father could not reach his traps. His heart had fallen. And when he visited the Bay store now, it was not to build credit but to draw from it. For as he could not tend his traps, he also could not hunt. And the little the government allowed us was hardly enough to live on. And our winter cache of meat was dwindling away. My father watched as his line of credit vanished from the book and the pen moved to another column. "I'm sorry, Krakoluk," the man said. But we had to eat. And my father had to feed his dogs. Then came the time when the cache of meat, caribou and seal, frozen on the roof of the house, was gone. And when Father went to the store, he went to borrow.

"It is a fine thing," my father said. "A man should have such a fine boat. A necessary thing. But not the most necessary thing." He was trying to make us all feel better.

He never showed a sad face. But we all knew how bad he felt inside. And when I went off to school, I would search the sky for Taktik, but always his face was covered with smoke-colored clouds. Clouds rushing fast out of the north. And the heavy snows and the bitter winds continued.

When finally the storms cleared, my father

again ran his traps. But by then the best of the season had passed. And he would need to work weeks simply to repay what he had borrowed. But my father pushed on. Setting even more traps. Adding days to his time on the tundra. Always quietly. Never complaining. But just as quietly, never accepting defeat. To the amazement of the man at the Bay store, my father cleared his debt, and again his credit started to build.

"You're not only bringing in more furs," the man told him, "but they are a better grade. With furs like these, I have to offer top price." And Father nodded with a smile. Though the storms had been a setback, the bitter cold had naturally thickened the fur of the white fox in a way they had not been for many seasons. And my father worked on. Running his traps for an even greater distance from the settlement. To the earth's frozen edge.

We had settled into the last dark month. Slowly Hekenjuk appeared on the horizon to take her place in the sky, just edging the snow-covered tundra with her light. On each return Father's dogsled was heavy with the fur of white fox. He was so close to having enough credit for the boat that he started to talk of what he would do when the sea ice melted. Then came word from the man at the Bay store that two other hunters, working together, had shown interest in buying the boat.

There was never anything in writing, my father was told. They never shook hands on the deal. It was still open to the best offer. "Sorry, Krakoluk." My father didn't understand that something had to be in writing. And he knew nothing of shaking hands.

Now, for several days, he did fall into a silent gloom. Collecting enough furs on his own was close to impossible. And we all assumed he had given up. But on the morning of the third day, I woke to find my father icing the runners of the *kamotik*. He put his dogs in harness and tied his old rifle to the sled. He worked seriously, quietly, as was his way.

Watching him, a certain pride swelled up inside of me. My father, this old Inuit, who had been half frozen on the open tundra time and time again, who had worked all winter only to be pushed back again, this Inuit had no intention of giving up. All of a sudden, I found myself running up to him just as his arm lifted to sound the whip above the dogs. "I will go with you!"

He looked at me skeptically.

"I can help!" I said.

Still he was skeptical. But I knew I could, and the words poured out as I explained to him. I could run the team. Tiitaa had taught me. Tiitaa taught me so many things.

He was thoughtful, then he nodded.

I ran back to the house to get my things. Rushing past my mother, with Siaja turning in surprise.

"I am going with Father!" I shouted.

Mother said nothing. She simply gathered my things into a bundle. Then as I started to run off, she called me back. She held out her knee-high sealskin socks and the heavy mukluks that pulled over them. With little thought, I almost grabbed them from her hands. But then I turned to offer her a thankful smile. Old Siaja was grinning so hard, she was showing her teeth. And then I was out of the little house and gone.

My father took the whip to the air, and the team pulled. Each dog took his weight, and the sled slipped over the frozen surface of the snow, gaining speed as we moved through the settlement. I settled on the *kamotik* with my bundle, watching Father's long whip trail over the snow then lift to cut the air as we crossed the low line of hills leaving Foster's Bay. I felt the good icy wind on my face and looked at the wide shoulders of my father as he sat on the sled with his back to me. He was relaxed, watching his team move smoothly, with the traces tight. I listened to the sound of the sled on the surface and the panting of the dogs. It was like old times. Before the settlement times. And the feeling of being totally free came back to me. And I felt as though the tundra were opening her arms to us.

We were four long days running Father's traps, and we took almost nothing. We built a snow house to shelter us during the sleeping hours, but always we were up much sooner than I wished and working again. I would wake to a cup of hot tea with a thick lump of seal fat floating on the surface. And porridge from the Bay store heavy with cream. Before I finished eating, my father would be putting the dogs in harness. I should have been awake much sooner, with the little stove heated and the food ready. But I could not clear my mind from sleep or get my body to move from the warmth of the blankets. Time in the settlement had changed me. But I tried and did what I could, though Father never said a word about my slowness, and after a time I woke to fill the teakettle with snow and help with the team.

Father was dismayed because we were taking no fox. Or so few. And after a passing of days we moved all the traps to another, far-off location. But still there was little to show for our work. Then a thought appeared to come over him. He looked at me strangely. Almost suspiciously. He said nothing. But I would learn much later that he determined that my spirit had something to do with the empty traps. Again Father was being put back through no fault of his own.

A morning came when I woke to find Father already gone. He had left one of the dogs for my protection and gone to run his line before the morning light. I couldn't understand why he hadn't taken me with him. And finally I blamed myself for sleeping so late and doing so little to help my father. My heart was heavy with guilt, and I was as unhappy as ever I have been through that long day. And late in the evening I climbed to a snow hill to watch for his return. I sat looking out over the great open tundra with the dog at my side. Out over the wild, free land.

It would be strange for some to believe that my spirit could keep the fox from the traps. But we Inuit believe such things. The Qallunaat do not understand them. But even today I know such things to be true. We Inuit believe that every natural thing on earth has a spirit. And that each has an effect on another. And any on all things. So my father believed that because I had put some of the Inuit ways behind me, had learned Qallunaat words and thoughts, I offended the spirit of the fox.

This is the way it was, and still, when Father returned that evening, he had nothing to show from his traps.

When I saw his team returning in the distance, I ran down to the snow house. When he came out of the cold, the warmth of the stove was waiting for him. I had tea ready and food cooked. He accepted all of this with a gentle smile as he settled back on the caribou hides that served as a floor. But after he had finished eating he said quietly, "We will sleep. Tomorrow we will return to Foster's Bay."

I looked at his tired face, and in a sad voice I said, "But we have taken almost nothing."

He nodded. "But still we will return to the settlement." Then he laid down to sleep.

I slept poorly that night. I woke often and lay in the darkness to look across at my father. I felt it was wrong to return to the settlement, but I knew that he knew things I did not. He was a great hunter and understood things. Unspoken things.

When dawn came I heated the stove for tea and food. We ate quietly. And after we finished eating I gathered our things to roll into the caribou hides to load on the *kamotik*. Outside I could hear the dogs barking excitedly. They were very loud, and I could tell by the sound of them that they were agitated. I knew Father had gone to take them from the gang line and slip them, one by one, into harness. But they sounded angry and threatening. And I did not hear the sound of the whip that would quiet them.

The snow bear was between my father and the dogs. The bear was up on his hind legs, and when I came out of the snow house, I looked straight up at him. Father shouted at me. "Maata! Run to the dogs!" And as he shouted the bear turned toward him.

I dropped the bundle and ran to the dogs, who were pulling wildly at the gang line.

"Turn them loose, Maata! Turn them loose!" Father's rifle was on the *kamotik*, and he could not reach it without passing under the paws of the bear. I reached the first dog and freed him. And just as quickly, the second and the third. By the time I reached the fourth, the first three huskies were tormenting the bear. Circling and snapping at him. Curling their lips angrily to show their teeth. I worked on down the line as fast as my hands could move until all eight dogs were free. And all eight huskies tightened their circle around the bear. Coming in at him from all directions.

A dog cried out in pain and limped across the snow, trailing blood. Another was thrown in the air to land near the *kamotik*, and he did not move. But still the dogs came. In a pack. Obeying the wolf instincts that had never left them. Working the bear in all directions. Six menacing dogs. Twelve feet of snow bear with his thousand pounds planted solidly. Then there came the single crack of a rifle, and the bear staggered. He turned slightly with the swing of a paw and went down.

First the dogs backed off. Then, with teeth showing, they started to move in again. First one. Then the others following. But the bear never moved. The dogs came in and would have torn the bear to shreds if my father's long whip hadn't cut the air above them. Still they did not back off. The wolf side of them still hot in their blood. But then the whip cracked, cutting an ear. And then another ear. And the dogs backed away.

We put the reluctant dogs back on the gang line. Father picked the injured dog up from the snow and laid him on the *kamotik*. One husky was dead, and Father took hold of his fur at the back of his neck. He dragged him far off from the others. My father would go back later to remove the skin and cut up the meat.

The bear was dead, and Father started right away to skin him. To remove the hide. He worked fast and quietly, before the Arctic cold started to freeze the flesh.

There was a smile on my father's face as he worked. I could not understand why. He had one dog killed and another badly hurt. He also could easily have been killed by the bear. And yet he worked with a smile. And after a time the words of a song came from his lips. I watched him and listened. He was praising the bear. Thanking him. Then my father looked at me and asked, "Do you know what we have, Maata? Do you know he is worth a hundred white fox?"

And then I understood. For the man at the Bay Company store would give much for the hide of such a bear.

My father had earned his boat.

June 1

Today Morgan lost a tooth. It was loose, and he pulled it right out of his mouth. He looked at it and me with troubled eyes. "It's getting much worse, Maata."

I didn't know how to reply. I told him, "The bay is still clearing. There is a wide channel now free of ice. And the wind has been coming off Tumak. Pushing the packs far out to sea."

He nodded. But I know he did not accept the little I offered.

When scurvy becomes advanced the teeth loosen. There is more swelling in the joints, and it is much more painful. Morgan has said nothing about the pain, but I know it is there; his ankles have swollen badly.

There is nothing I can do for Morgan. There is nothing I can give him. There is not even a medical book I can read from, and I know so little. No medicines in little bottles. No vitamin pills. All of that went in the fire.

I wish I knew Pavvik's healing song. His spirit song. But I don't even know the language of the shaman.

We Inuit believe all humans have three souls.

Our name-soul is given to us at birth and can be passed on to another. The free-soul that is with us is an immortal spirit and will live on after death in another world. And last, our life-soul. Our life-soul suffers as we do and dies with us. Pavvik would say that Morgan is suffering from a loss of his life-soul, and Pavvik would work to bring it back. There is always cause for a loss of soul. A breaking of taboos or a bad spirit. Pavvik would search this out. But I can think of no taboo Morgan has broken. Or of any spirit who would make him suffer.

Daniel Morgan is a good and decent man. He cried when Olson died. He didn't know I saw him. But I saw the tears in his eyes. He cries still in his heart for his friend.

If there was a bad spirit, I think it was that spirit who started the fire. And I think it was the moody Smith who brought that spirit down on us.

We never knew how the fire started. But Smith had been in the cabin alone for most of that day. Smith was a man who studied rocks. What Webster's book calls a *geologist*. Smith could sit for hours going over the rocks he had brought in. He would scatter them out on the table and study them in the light of the lamp. He would adjust the glasses on his nose and make long notes in his book. Sometimes he would let a meal go cold or only pick at it just to work on his rocks. It seemed the only time he was happy, or at least not moody.

All rocks are the same to me. On the tundra only the snow is different. But Smith could read things from rocks. He once told Nicolson that Tumak was a young island. That it was formed in the last ice age. At a time when the ice was a mile thick and slowly moving down from the top of the world. He knew this from his rocks. And he looked over his glasses and waited for Nicolson's reply. All Nicolson said was, "Interesting." But I think Nicolson believed him, even though he acted as if he didn't want to be bothered.

I didn't believe Smith. And when he left his rocks scattered on the table, I would have to clear them away. I needed the table space for cooking, and the men needed a place to eat. Once, I got so angry I threw them out the door of the cabin. When he found what I had done, he complained to Morgan. But Morgan only shook his head and told Smith he should be more organized. "Find a place for your work and keep it there."

"It is evident the girl doesn't like me!" said Smith. "But please tell her to leave my things alone!"

Morgan said nothing. Still shaking his head he simply walked away.

I watched from the cabin window as Smith searched for his rocks. When he came back in he gave me a very dark look, and he didn't talk to me for days. After that he found a place in the corner to store them. Later Morgan told me I should be more patient with Smith. That much of the expedition was built around his work. That his rocks and his notes were very important. I said I would try.

I once heard Morgan tell Olson that the research Smith was doing was very significant to the government. Even more valuable than Nicolson's study of the weather, or their own mapping of the surrounding country.

"He is searching for certain minerals," Morgan explained. "Especially cryolite."

"What is cryolite?" Olson asked.

Morgan shrugged his shoulders. "I'm not real sure. But according to Smith it's very rare," he said. "They use it in manufacturing aluminum for airplanes and things like that. And the only large deposit and working mine in the world is in Greenland." But, along with the cryolite, Smith had been told to look for other things, Morgan added. Metals such as nickel, copper, or even uranium.

I didn't know why all of these things were so important, but I tried very hard to be patient with Smith and his rocks. I tried because Morgan had asked me.

Nicolson was not patient with Smith. He simply tried to avoid him as much as possible. Often, when they ate at the table, no more than a few words would pass between them.

"He has always aggravated me," Nicolson said. "The last expedition I was on, there was Smith, myself, and four others. Besides our research, we all had our chores, just keeping up the camp. But Smith seldom did anything to help. All he knows is his rocks."

When Nicolson learned how I had thrown the rocks out the cabin door a slight grin formed at the corner of his mouth. But he said nothing.

The fire started near the little stove we used to warm the cabin. Smith always built the fire up in the stove until the iron glowed red from the heat. Morgan told him not to build it so high. But Smith was always complaining about the cold, and he would keep adding wood. "It's too cold," Smith would say.

"Damn!" Morgan would tell him. "It's the Arctic. What did you expect? And if you use up our supply of wood, you'll know what real cold is."

But that didn't stop Smith.

On the day of the fire I was down by the sea ice. Morgan and Olson were across the island with the dog team. And Nicolson had gone out to measure the wind. Nicolson had funny little cups on a long pole that spun from the force of the wind. He would go out each day if he was not away with the dog team. If he was away, Morgan or Olson would go for him and make notes in a book. On this day the wind was very strong. Coming off the sea and across Tumak. Freezing the surface of the snow.

We all saw the smoke. I saw it, and I saw Nicolson running back toward the cabin. The smoke was low across the island and pulling away fast in the wind. But there was a lot of smoke. And then I saw the glow of the fire. And I saw Smith running about excitedly. Then he turned and saw Nicolson and started shouting. But the wind took away his words, and I don't know what he was shouting.

I reached the cabin at the same time Morgan and Olson came up with the dog team. Morgan pushed his way in through the smoke. The flames were leaping high in the air and the wind was breaking them off. Then Morgan came out again, coughing and choking, with fire clinging to his parka and mittens. Nicolson and Olson pushed him down in the snow and rolled him over to put the fire out. Olson took out his knife to cut the mittens from Morgan's hands. Nicolson was pulling off Morgan's parka. It was still smoldering. I remember how Morgan looked up at Smith, who was standing above him with a stunned look on his face. Smith stood as if he were paralyzed.

"The maps. The work." I heard Morgan say. Then he turned away. His eyes fixed on the fire.

Then Olson was moving. That fast, Olson had gone through the burning doorway and was lost in the thick smoke.

Nicolson called after Olson. Morgan tried to get up. It couldn't have been a full minute, and the flames just boiled into the sky through the roof. I fell to my knees in the snow. Then came a roar. I looked up to see the walls of the cabin falling in and the roof sinking down. The flames shot up, and hot embers swept off in the wind. I lowered my head and covered my eyes.

There was an angry spirit there, I believe. A bad spirit. Perhaps it was in the rocks who did not want their story to be told. Perhaps it was in the fire. I think it followed Smith. But it should have gone away with Smith. With Smith and Nicolson over the winter tundra.

Daniel Morgan is a good and decent man. He should not suffer so.

June 4

The ice floats like little islands in the bay. I saw a seagull far out over the water. But I have found none nesting yet on the island. Like the geese, the seagulls appear to be flying north, passing over Tumak. Perhaps they have found a better nesting place. Perhaps we have disturbed Tumak too much. We have left our mark on it.

Some of the stones Smith collected were taken from the graves of the ancient ones. I did not know this then. Much later, when I found the graves, I saw that the bones were exposed to the wind.

When Siaja was a child there lived with her people a shaman who could go back through the winters to visit the ancient ones. She told me the story. She gave the words to me as the ancient ones gave them to the shaman. It was told that they came from the land where Hekenjuk sleeps.

Far to the west. Over the ice and frozen tundra in search of food. They traveled to the east, where Hekenjuk starts her day. They were the first in this land. This land we now call Nunavut. Our land. Land of the Inuit. And for a thousand winters they lived in this place because it was rich with game and the spirits were kind. They hunted caribou and seal and white bear. They took fish from the sea and small whales. And even now their stone tent rings and graves can be found. And their *inukshuks* stand in lonely places across the tundra. Little stone men looking silently over the frozen land.

Life was good to the ancient ones, Siaja said, until bad spirits came. Until their hunters lost respect for the land and the game. The winters grew longer. Then hunger came. And their people died. And those who did not die moved farther north still. Far up over the top of the ice, where they now dance in the lights that tie the night sky to the earth.

I took Siaja's words and put them on paper. And when I showed the pages to Mr. Sanders, he was excited. "Maata, you are a proficient writer!" he said. "You have captured the true feeling of the old myths."

I went home and looked up the word *proficient* in Mr. Webster's large book. When I found it I was pleased. When I showed the pages to Siaja she asked me to read them. As I read them there was a gleam in her eyes. When I finished she said, "Now the pages have a spirit. Now I understand. Books have spirits." Siaja was very happy.

All of this happened only days before Siaja died. Before her breathing ended.

I did not wake that morning and go to Siaja. I did not listen for her breathing. Mother was the first to find her. My mother, who always woke up long before I did. And my mother came to my sleeping place and woke me gently. Woke me to tell me the old woman had gone.

I rubbed the sleep from my eyes and pushed the hair from my face. In the beginning I did not understand my mother's words. Then she put her arm around my shoulders. The old woman had gone. She repeated it several times. Her free-soul was in the spirit world.

I looked over at Siaja, who was on her sleeping place covered with warm blankets. Then I realized.

I pulled free of Mother and went to Siaja. I put my head on her chest, but she was not breathing.

I shook her hard, but still there was nothing. "Siaja!"

As I cried the tears washed over Siaja's cold face. I took a corner of the blanket to wipe them away, but still Siaja did not move.

I turned away.

I went to my mother's arms, and she pulled me close and held me there.

Siaja's free-soul was in the spirit world, beyond the words of the shaman. Where only the wind goes. Mother tried to make me understand. But it was difficult.

chapter five

They made a place for Siaja on the hill above
Foster's Bay. A place near Lisi. Father, with help
from Morgan and Olson, gathered the stones to
cover the grave. They buried with her a fine *ulu*,
a woman's knife, and a set of sewing needles.
Mother quietly placed them near Siaja's hands.

I had nothing to give Siaja, and in that I was
most sorry. She had given me so much. So much
love. And she had taught me so much. But I made
a promise in my heart as they placed the last
stones. I promised I would one day give her the

only gift I could. I would give her words. When I learned to give sorrow words. When I learned to give love words. I would put Siaja's spirit in a book.

When Siaja went away it was a dark and lonely time. But I didn't know how lonely it could be. Not long after, Morgan and Olson left Foster's Bay. Olson returned to his home in Montreal. And Morgan went back to the United States. To a place called Boston. Morgan showed me this place on a map, but I did not understand the distance. And I did not know I would not see him again for several years.

I hoped Tiitaa would come before the snows melted in the spring. But there was no Tiitaa. And spring seemed to come and go so quickly that year. Always, each day, I missed Siaja. And big, gentle Olson. And Morgan. In summer Father seemed to be in love with his boat and spent more time at sea than at home. It didn't appear to bother my mother, who always had some way of keeping busy. I waited impatiently for the new school year.

There was a war in Europe. But I didn't know much about that. I didn't know until Mr. Sanders also left Foster's Bay that spring. He came to our little house to say good-bye, for I had become his favorite student. "I'll be back when it's over, Maata. But you keep working on those lessons."

He said I had a real gift for words and the day would come when that gift would serve me well. "You've got to promise me," he said.

I promised, though feeling an emptiness at his leaving.

The *Venture* came into the bay a few days later. She came in to resupply the Hudson's Bay Company store. The *Venture* was much bigger than the *North Wind*. Higher in the water and longer on the horizon. Father used his boat to carry supplies to the shore. It was the first Qallunaat money, real money and not credit, that he had ever earned.

Mr. Sanders got a ride out to the *Venture* with Father, and that was the last I ever saw of him. I heard some men talking, and they said that the army would never take Mr. Sanders. He was too old and his eyes were bad. Not like Morgan and Olson, who were probably in France already. I knew nothing of France and thought it was near Boston. Or perhaps close to Montreal. I did not learn about Europe and France and the Great War until much later at the boarding school in Quebec

City. There I saw books that had maps in them. I would learn how wrong I was. But the men talking were also wrong. The army did take Mr. Sanders, and that autumn he was killed in Europe.

We Inuit know almost nothing of war. And in 1918 very little news reached that far north. So life in Foster's Bay moved on as always, dictated by the changes of seasons, by the wind from the north. By birth and death. By the number of sled dogs a man had. By how many sets of traps he would work. By the supply ships that brought in goods and took out furs.

The *Venture* came again late that summer when the snow had already fallen and ice was forming in the bay. It was an early cold and the ice solid enough for the men to haul the supplies in by dogsled, running from the ship over the ice and right up over the snow-covered tundra. I walked far out over the sea ice to see the size of the great ship. A great iron monster with her hull rising like a mountain. And two stacks exhaling black smoke. She had broken through the new ice effortlessly, but the ice had formed again, tight against her iron skin. She was so high, I could not see the men on her deck, only the cargo being lowered down to the hunters waiting with their teams. She cast a long dark shadow on the blue ice, and the men worked in the cold of it.

The *Venture* unloaded cargo and two passengers. One was the teacher the government had sent up to replace Mr. Sanders. A little man by the name of Walden. I remember he had a large nose, red from the cold, and small eyes. His head seemed too big for his body. And when they lowered him from the deck of the *Venture* to the ice below, he had a frightened look on his face.

Following him down was the Reverend Moorehead. A bigger man than Walden. He showed no concern as he was lowered to the waiting teams. He was relaxed, but there was something stern about him. His feet had no sooner hit the ice than he turned to Walden. "Here at last," he announced, sounding both impatient and pleased.

I was standing very close, and he looked directly at me and smiled, as if his words were meant especially for me.

Walden rubbed his red nose and sniffled. He looked across the ice at the settlement. At the low group of houses with the smoke pulling off the tundra. Bleak and gray under a lead sky. "Here," he agreed cheerlessly. "All this for a few Indians."

"Eskimos," Moorehead corrected. "Not Indians. Eskimos."

"Same difference. Savages. I'm expected to teach savages."

"If it's so distasteful, why did you come?"

"Contract," said the teacher. He explained that he had a one-year contract. The money was good, and it also kept him out of the war. "And you?"

"I have a contract with God," said the reverend.

Walden nodded. But he didn't appear impressed.

Father asked me later who the two Qallunaat were.

I told Father the little one was the new teacher. And the big one a Christian shaman.

Father said he didn't like them. The little one was like a sick seal. The big one like a hungry bear. Then he asked what the Christian wanted of us.

"To give us a new spirit."

"I have three now," said my father. "I do not need another."

When our school opened a few weeks later, I faced Mr. Walden for the first time. Our past lessons had gone far beyond the work he assigned us those first days. I tried to explain, but he cut me short. "Mr. Sanders had his way of teaching and I have mine," he said.

I explained that Mr. Sanders often allowed me to work far ahead of the others. And at times work with the other students.

"I know where this class should be. And that's exactly where you will be," Mr. Walden told me. He added that he would not have some Eskimo child who cut her teeth on seal fat telling him how to start the year. That I should be grateful just to have a teacher. "Now, sit down!"

I went sadly into the school year. And after those first days I never so much as offered to answer a question in class. I did secretly, quietly, read through the books given us. But after that school became a chore, not a pleasure.

The Reverend Moorehead showed far more interest in his work than did our teacher. He opened his mission church in one of the small box houses in the settlement. And he went to visit each family. He ate our food and spoke our language. And he explained that God had sent him to other settlements, where he had left an established church in each. He gave all his sermons in Inuktitut. And to a small group he taught Christian hymns, translating the words from English. At times, when the winter winds were not wild on the tundra, we would hear the singing from the small church. I would see my father listening carefully. "Not bad," he would say. "Almost a fine thing. But they should have the drum sound. It is nothing if they do not have the drum sound."

When the Reverend Moorehead came to visit us, we all listened to his words. My father brought frozen caribou meat from the roof of the house. And my mother made tea and offered muktuk while the meat was thawing on the lamp. Muktuk is the outer skin of the beluga whale and is a special treat. The Reverend Moorehead ate with us and laughed with us, and then he said to Father, "I am told you sing to the drum like no other hunter in Foster's Bay."

My father's face glowed as his teeth clamped down on a piece of muktuk, and he cut it away with his knife. He chewed and swallowed and said easily, "I know many hunting songs."

"It would give us pleasure if you would learn our songs. Our people sing well. But we need the sound of the drum."

"This is true," said Father. Then he said, "I will give this thought."

So my father did go to the church of the Christian shaman. But Mother showed no interest in it. And I went only once to hear my father sing to the sound of the drum.

It was not a most happy time for me. And still there were far more lonely times to come.

June 8

Morgan was outside today. I went across the island looking for gulls' eggs, but I found nothing. When I came back Morgan was sitting in the sun. I made a cup of hot tea and brought it to him. He asked if I had been to Olson's grave. I told him I had fixed the stones and little cross that same morning.

He said he was thinking about Olson. Thinking a lot about him. Then he drank the tea and was quiet. Later he asked, with a slight chance of voice, "Are you keeping a cartridge in that rifle?"

"Yes."

"Too many bears," he said. "Too damn many bears."

We both knew that more bears would be coming ashore as the ice melted. I told him I saw another that morning. I saw him crossing the far side of the island.

He shook his head. He was quiet a long time, thinking. He drank the tea quietly.

After a long time I offered to make him another cup of tea, but he didn't reply. Finally I took the empty cup from his hands. His fingers fell away and rested on the blanket that covered his legs. I could see how tired he was. He looked at the sea ice floating in the bay. "What we need now is Krakoluk and that old boat of his," he reflected. A slight smile appeared on his lips. "Your father sure did love that boat. Didn't he, Maata?"

I said nothing.

"He would go places with that boat that the *Venture* wouldn't dare go."

"Yes," I said.

"Old Krakoluk, he had more courage than most men I've known. Deep and honest." He laughed slightly. But he didn't say what he was thinking about. Just old thoughts drifting. Then he turned to me. "I sure did like your father. And your mother. Nua was a fine woman. I was very sorry when I heard what happened."

I turned from him to watch the thin clouds above the bay.

"You don't talk about it, Maata. You should talk about it. It's good to talk about things. It helps."

I turned away from Morgan and went into the cabin. I didn't want to talk about it.

June 9

The wind spoke and my father listened. The wind moved over the ice floes and rippled the surface of the black water in the narrow leads. In some places the leads were so narrow, Father had to ease the boat through. There was a worried look on his face, his lips were tight and quiet.

A white mist rolled like heavy smoke just above the ice and the water. The boat drifted almost like magic through the veil. The sound of the engine was hard and low, only an idle, above the solid silence of the water. We slipped between the floes. Between cakes of ice as thick as the boat. So quietly, almost with reverence.

My father listened. And the wind whispered.

Moorehead turned nervously. There was nothing to see in the mist. It was Father's quiet, his listening, that made Moorehead tense. Twice Moorehead spoke, but my father held up his hand for silence.

All the sea and all that was on the sea was in motion. The black water, the ice, the boat, and us in it. All travelers together.

I moved closer to my mother, and she put her arm around my shoulders for comfort.

It was quiet for so long, and then came the first

loud boom of crashing ice. It came out of the white mist from the distance. A lead closing suddenly.

I saw Moorehead's lips moving. He was making a prayer.

A draft of ice-cold air crossed the water, disturbing the mist. Father listened, turning in that direction. It was only a whisper, but my father took every word.

"I should have listened to you," Moorehead said softly. But Father gave no reply.

Moorehead moved closer to my father. They were almost shoulder to shoulder. Moorehead listened as my father did. But Moorehead didn't hear the wind.

We had crossed the bay that morning to where a small camp had been set up. The sea had been free of ice then and smooth like a black mirror, gentle and easy. But in the afternoon the ice had started to move in. Big floes coming into the bay with a shift in the wind. Moving slowly. Filling the black water. Crowding into the bay. And Father watched them, walking down to his boat. Watching them carefully.

It was late June, time for salmon trout and char, and several families had moved across the bay to set up a fishing camp near the mouth of a small river. Their caribou-hide tents lined the shore, and the smoke of their fires bent low under the blue sky. The men fished with throw lines using lures of polished ivory. Some went far out on the rocks to spear the fish with their three-pronged leisters. In places between the rocks the icy waters boiled white with fish, with the silver flash of char and the soft gold of the trout fighting the stream. Small groups of women and older children cleaned the fish and laid them to dry while the youngest children ran and played, filling the air with laughter. Mother and I helped with the cleaning and were rewarded with the roe our fingers pulled from the pink stomachs. The roe was sweet and strong and icy cold.

The Reverend Moorehead mingled with the people. A hunter allowed him the use of a throw line, and the fish were so plentiful that even the reverend pulled them in. Then Moorehead made his way far out on the rocks and was just as successful with the leister as he had been with the throw line. The people respected the skill of this Qallunaaq and praised him. He laughed with them and joined their circle to eat slices of fresh char and salmon trout roe. And he told the story of a man called Peter. A story from the Bible book.

And all this time the ice was drifting into the bay on the black currents. My father came to the reverend and said, "We should leave now. It is not good to wait."

"Soon," Moorehead replied. "Soon."

And later Father said, "It must be now or we should stay until the bay is clear."

"Yes," Moorehead replied. "Very soon. I will finish my story and we will go."

And my father was patient. He had grown to trust Moorehead, and he was fond of him. My father had taken a place in the little church and there sang to the sound of the drum. And he and the reverend had traveled all along the coast in the Peterhead boat, visiting the hunting camps and the fishing camps. Moorehead had never shown fear and had always endured the worst of things without complaining. "A fine man," my father often said. But on this day he worried. And when Moorehead finished with the people and made his way to the boat where Mother and I waited, I heard my father say, "It is best to wait now until the bay is clear."

But Moorehead insisted we could make it safely. He could see open channels. And he told Father that God would watch over us.

"You must listen to the wind," said Father.

Moorehead insisted. We would cross safely.

And so, reluctantly, my father worked the small boat out between the ice floes into an open channel. And the channel was clear for a great distance. But then even I knew the wind had shifted. We could see the settlement and soon would have reached shore when the white mist rolled over the sea and ice packs. The wind had shifted against the black currents, and the ice was in turmoil.

The wind picked up, and one great block of ice scraped against another. And now the sea was starting to swell, and the water was no longer quiet. The boat bumped off one block of ice, and another moved toward us. When I looked at Moorehead he was troubled and his lips were white. I felt Mother's arm tighten on my shoulders. And then it happened. We were pounded and the boat lifted. My father went into the sea. Mother's arm was gone from my shoulders. A large floe of blue ice lifted up and up, taking the boat with it. Dumping us out and smashing down violently. There was a shattering roar, and the boat was in pieces.

I tumbled out onto the ice. Then the floe started to shift again, and I was sliding down to the black water. The water was churning up shattered pieces of the boat. Ice was grinding against ice. Then I felt a hand take mine and pull me back. I saw the pale face of Moorehead as he reached out his other hand. Then the floe settled against another, and there was nothing but the ice and the wind and the sea.

My father and mother were gone.

I screamed so hard, I shattered the wind.

I searched the dark water and the floes. I searched until Moorehead locked me in his arms and held me there. "There is nothing!" he yelled. "Nothing!" And I fought Moorehead until I could fight no more. "Nothing," he said again, gently. And my heart sank and my legs were weak and all my world dark.

June 13

Today the sun was so warm, I felt the heat of it on my face. And I found small shoots of heather in a split of rock. The patches of snow are melting away. And the fox is losing his winter coat.

Today I went to the place where the ancient ones lived. Where Smith had gathered many of his rocks. Where the stone circles of their tents can still be found. And where there was a burial place, I gathered stones and rebuilt it so their bones would not be exposed to the wind and the rain. I told their spirits to rest safely, and I thanked them for allowing us time on Tumak. It was their island long before it was our island, though I am sure by another name. My father said that we must always respect the place of others before us. Those who made the passage before we did.

I sang to the wind one of my father's old songs. My voice is soft, and I did not have a drum to follow. But the words offered comfort to the ancient ones and regard for this land we can Nunavut.

> *Keewatin?* North Wind?
> Carry my words over the silent stones
> and blue ice.
> Lift the wings of the raven who brought
> light to the world.
> For in his flight the shadow of his wings
> sweeps over the ancient bones.
> And tell them it is the same
> land without change.
> And the same we will leave
> for those who follow.
> The tundra and the sea, Nunavut,

In good keeping through our passage.
Assure them.
And let their spirits sleep beneath the
blankets of white.

It would have been a fine thing if my father had sung it. His voice could lift the wind and bend it and divide it. "Hai-ee-ya, hai-ee-ya!" Bending to the dance and the beat of the drum. Dancer on the wind. The spirits knew the voice of Krakoluk the hunter. And I think he dances still beyond the sea and distant clouds. At times I think I hear his voice and the rhythm of his drum. The voice of a good man with quiet courage who loved the place of his passage.

June 15

Moorehead and the officials at Foster's Bay made arrangements for me to go away to a boarding school in Quebec City. There was no one to take care of me. And I think that Moorehead felt he had some responsibility to me and believed he was doing the right thing. There were families we had been close to, but times were difficult for them.

Though it was never said, I know I would have been a burden. I kept wishing during those weeks before my departure south that Tiitaa would return. But there was no Tiitaa and no way of finding him. He was free on the tundra. And with the small band of Inuit in a far distant world from mine.

So arrangements were made and Moorehead said, "You will like it there, Maata. It is a good place. There will be many girls your age. And you will have a chance for a real education." And he added, "And God will keep you safe."

I had little to say in the matter. So at the age of twelve, in the early summer of 1919, with a small bundle of clothes and a few Canadian dollars Moorehead had given me, I boarded the great ship *Venture* for the long trip south.

Though the *Venture* was a much larger ship, conditions on her, for us Inuit, were little better than on the *North Wind*. It was dark and gloomy inside the lower level of the ship. There were portholes on either side, but they offered little light off the dark sea. In one, large open-space beds, like bunk beds, were fastened to the wall. In a corner, behind a wall, was one flush toilet. There was a sink. And in the center of the room, a long table with benches.

There were no white people on the lower level. All the Qallunaat traveled on the upper deck, which was clean and painted white with comfortable little cabins. Only we Inuit were crowded in below. Few were going as far south as I was. As far as Quebec City. Most were moving from one settlement to another. A few had the sickness, tuberculosis, and were going to the hospital in Cambridge Sound. These people were kept at the far end of our sleeping place, though they ate with us almost every day.

For the first week the weather was miserable, the sea rough and stormy, and many people were sick. Their sickness fouled the stale air. I did not get sick, though I don't know why. Each day we were given two meals. For breakfast it was always porridge and dry toast and a weak tea. In the evening it was meat and boiled potatoes. Always the same, never different. In the beginning some were too sick to eat. And later many didn't want to eat anyway. But I forced myself to take the food, for Mother had always told me how important food was.

It was cold and damp. On the tundra the cold is a very dry cold. It was the dampness I could not adjust to, and often I would wear all the clothes I had brought with me. But still the dampness would creep into my bones and send chills through my body. There was a heater near our sleeping place, with pipes that ran through the floor. When the person closest to the heat left the ship, I moved my sleeping place. A bottom bunk near the heater. But the heater made so much noise, the pipes banging, that often it was impossible to sleep. And still I was cold. On those days when the sun broke through the clouds, I would go to the upper deck to warm myself. But those days were few.

The journey from Foster's Bay to Quebec City took several months. The *Venture* traveled far north before it turned south again, leaving Hudson Bay through Hudson Strait to round Newfoundland and finally enter the Gulf of Saint Lawrence. During that time we stopped at almost every settlement along the coast.

It was October when finally we entered the Saint Lawrence River. Through a thin fog, I could see the land washed with trees and green, rolling hills climbing up away from the river. There was just a hint of red and gold with the coming of autumn. Little houses were tucked in along the riverbank. I stood at the rail on the upper deck for hours. It was all so beautiful and yet so lonely. For

I was on my own and a long way from home.

When we docked at the pier in Quebec City, all around us were ships, some much bigger than the *Venture*. And there were tall buildings of brick and stone. There were crowds of people gathered on the pier. I had never seen so many people at one time in one place. More people than in all of Foster's Bay. Some shouted up to the passengers on the *Venture*. And they all frightened me, for I thought I could become lost in such a sea of people. So I held tight to the rail as others were leaving the ship.

When almost all had left the ship I was still standing alone. Then I saw a man and a woman coming toward me. The woman looked down at me and smiled, but her face was stern, and there was no real warmth in her smile. "You must be Maata," she said.

"Yes," I told her, and I could hear my voice quavering.

She turned to the man. "John, take the child's bundle." The man moved obediently at her command. The woman turned to me and took my hand in hers. "Come along," she ordered. "We have a long ride before us. And I would like to get back before nightfall." She started off, almost pulling me along the deck. I looked back over my shoulder to see the man following at a distance.

"We expected you weeks ago," the woman said. "We understood you were changing ships at Frobisher Bay. This whole thing has been mixed up. You should have changed ships, you know. Did you know that, child?"

I shook my head. I was trying to keep pace with her and listen at the same time. She made it clear that I had caused a lot of aggravation. As she spoke she called back for the man to hurry along. Then to me she said, "My name is Mrs. Colville. I will expect you always to use 'Mrs. Colville' when addressing me. Do you understand, child?"

Before I could reply she continued.

"We will find you another name." A Christian name, she said. Maata would never do. She looked down at me again. "And how long have you been wearing those clothes, child? Have you been weeks in the same clothes? Do you have lice? When did you bathe last?" Then she called back for John.

It was my first ride in an automobile. I was put in the back with Mrs. Colville. The man, John, drove. I sat clutching my small bundle on my lap. My heart was pounding with fear and excitement.

We passed buildings, tall buildings, and people. So many people. Other automobiles passed us, going fast. Mrs. Colville continued talking. But I wasn't listening. We left the city and there were trees. And there were more trees, and we were following a trail along the river. And Mrs. Colville was saying, "We will call you Sarah. Sarah is a good name. You may keep Maata if you like. But here you will be called Sarah."

We went up a hill, high above the river. The trees were spaced out, and they were large. Before us was a great house of gray stone. It filled all the top of the hill.

Mrs. Colville patted my hand, "Welcome home, Sarah."

June 17

A sudden freeze. The bay is locked in ice again. The wind has been blowing for two days. For two days the sun has been hidden away. Lost behind dark clouds rolling out of the north. I saw flakes of snow pass the window. This is June, but it is like winter again. It can't last. I know it can't last. And I keep telling Morgan it's only a passing thing. He looks at me but says nothing.

I trimmed Morgan's hair and helped him shave his beard away. His face is hollow. He is pale and feeble. The old lines, once smile lines, are deep scars now. He has lost several more teeth. He is always thirsty and asking for water. And when he sleeps he holds fevered conversations.

I know this freeze will not last. Hekenjuk will return and warm the earth again.

In the afternoon I put on my warm clothes and took the rifle and went out into the storm. I went down to look at the sea running white and black and angry. There were thin floes of ice smashing one into another. The waves tore at the rocky beach as if trying to tear it from the earth. But still the sea is free, and even this freeze will not lock it in again. And the ship will come to take us away. It must come.

It must come soon.

chapter six

~ *June 20, 1924* ~

Morgan woke me from my sleeping place. "Get the rifle," he said anxiously. "And give me the shotgun."

I pushed back the warm blankets and looked at him with sleepy eyes. Then I could hear the bear breathing and sniffing on the other side of the cabin door. Then the bear put his weight on the door, and the door moaned. And then it was quiet.

I rolled out of my sleeping place and got the shotgun and gave it to Morgan. He had pulled himself up in a sitting position, away from the little window but facing the door. He asked for the shells.

I passed him the box of twelve-gauge shells. He opened the box and spilled the shells out before him. Then he opened the shotgun and filled the chambers. He snapped the gun closed.

There was a scratching sound at the door and then the weight of the bear. I could hear the bear sniffing along the edge of the door. In my mind I could picture the big white bear up on his hind legs, his breath steaming the air, his nose searching for small cracks in the wood.

I took the rifle down from the wall and quietly worked the bolt, pushing a long cartridge into the chamber. I left the safety off. Then I moved far back from the door. My hands were shaking. I could hear Morgan's voice in a whisper, telling me not to shoot unless he broke through. We don't want to wound him. We don't need any wounded bears on the island. I understood, looking at Morgan in the dim glow of the iron stove. Thinking more about my shaking hands. Morgan said the bear was just curious and would probably move off in a little while. Bears were like that. He might go away.

I nodded my head. But I didn't believe it.

Suddenly the door shook violently, and I jumped. The wood shuddered on the flimsy hinges. At the same instant Morgan was lifting the shotgun.

The door quivered. Then, again, it was quiet.

Morgan looked at me. He was very calm. I tried to swallow, but my throat was dry. I ran my tongue over my lips.

It was quiet for a long time. We waited. Listening. I knew he was still there. I could feel him there on the other side. I looked at Morgan, and I knew Morgan could feel him.

Then the door bulged inward. It appeared to bend at the top. The bear throwing his entire weight against it. A thousand pounds of curiosity.

Morgan was lifting the shotgun higher.

A white paw slipped through the opening, and the long claws dug at the wood. Then the bear's nose was working its way in. The wood was bending. The door was giving.

I pulled the rifle into my shoulder. "I'll shoot him!" I said. "Shoot straight, rifle!"

"How the hell can you miss?" Morgan asked.

The wood was cracking.

"Now?" I said.

"No," Morgan said.

I waited for the time it took to take a deep breath. "Now?"

"No," he said again.

I lowered the rifle, very scared but very annoyed. I put the rifle on the table, showing my anger. There was a large iron pot hanging near the stove. I lifted it with both hands by the long handle. As I turned I saw the look of surprise on Morgan's face.

I stepped to the door, swinging the pot in the air just as the bear's head was coming through. I hit the nose. *Smack!* A real smack! And I heard the bear groan. The nose pulled back, but I hit it a second time before it was gone. I heard the bear growl in pain. It was almost a cry. Almost sad. I swung for the paw, but the paw had slipped away, and I hit the door solidly. There was another groan. Then a growl. I waited, holding the pot up over my head. It was quiet. Still I waited, ready with the pot. There was nothing. I looked at Morgan. "Gone," I said.

"Gone," said Morgan. There was a look of total astonishment on his face.

I lowered the pot in my shaking hands. "Maybe he will be back," I said.

"No bear is that big a fool," Morgan said. And

then he laughed. He laughed the way Morgan used to laugh.

"I hit him with a smack," I said.

"You're a hell of a girl, Maata." And after more laughter he said, "I think you can put the guns away. But keep the pot." And then he was laughing with tears in his eyes.

June 22

Today it was clear again. The storm gone. Hekenjuk throws her warmth on the earth. Little shoots of green start to appear on the tundra. Soon there will be flowers and other growing things. Even the wind off the sea is pleasant now. And the sea quiet and smooth.

I went to Olson's grave and spent a long time there, sitting on the rocks, looking out at the wide ocean. I told Olson about the bear and how Morgan had laughed. Olson said it is good for Morgan to laugh. And I told Olson when the flowers come to the tundra, I will bring some to show him.

Olson was a man who could love flowers. He had a spirit that made flowers important. That made all things important. And all equal. I once told him that we Inuit believe all things have a spirit. That all are related. And he replied, "Of course they are." He said it so easily. As if there were never a question. "Of course they are." It is understood.

I miss my friend Olson badly. I spent much time with him today.

When I returned to the cabin Morgan was in a sad mood again. Later, in a half sleep, he was delirious. He tossed and turned and talked about Boston, that faraway place, though I couldn't understand what he was saying. Beads of sweat rolled off his face, and his lips were dry. I wiped his face with a damp cloth and gave him some water to drink. Then I held his hand as he went into a quiet sleep.

Morgan was so different a few days ago. He seemed stronger then. But each time he appears stronger, the sickness comes back and washes his body of strength. It can only be a few weeks before the ship comes. If he can last a few weeks.

June 23

Mrs. Colville was shocked to find that I could both read and write the Qallunaat language. And she was not as difficult a person as she made herself out to be. Though she was never completely friendly.

The school was clean and orderly. My sleeping place was in a long room where the beds were lined in two rows. A small chest fit under each bed, and there we kept our personal things. Each morning our beds had to be made just perfectly, and each morning Mrs. Colville or one of her assistants made an inspection. They put a mark in a little book if something was not in order. And when a girl got too many marks, she was given a task no other wanted, like cleaning the flush toilets or working in the laundry or scouring pots in the kitchen. Only in that way could a girl make the book clean again.

I received two marks the first morning when I stood for inspection barefoot, my hair hanging long and wild down my back. I would have received more marks, but one of the French-Canadian girls hurriedly made up my bed for me.

"You must learn from the beginning," Mrs. Colville said. "Sarah," she told her assistant with the book. "Give her two points." Then her steel eyes flashed over me. "We have rules. Absolute rules," she warned.

We all ate in a big room close to the kitchen, on the first floor, near the garden. I liked this room because the light from Hekenjuk filled it in the morning and there were large doors that opened to the outside when the weather was good.

For five days of the week, after breakfast, we were given four hours of schooling. We were divided into groups according to our age and how advanced each of us was in our lessons. I was moved through two groups in the first few weeks.

After the morning school we all had work to do, some task assigned us, which lasted into the evening. And after dinner we had two hours for school lessons until bedtime. This schedule differed only on Saturday and Sunday. Saturday was a day for laundry and bathing. And on Sunday Mrs. Colville gathered us in the big room to read from the Bible book after breakfast. After the reading we had a few free hours of our own.

In time I learned from some of the girls that I was very fortunate to be in Mrs. Colville's Boarding School. Some had been in other places that were not so good. And though Mrs. Colville could be very strict, she applied the same rules to all. And in ways, she could be just as kind and understanding. But still I was lonely for my home in the north.

My bed in the dormitory was the last in the row below the windows. The lights went out at nine o'clock each night. In the darkness some of the girls would laugh and giggle, tell stories, or just carry on until someone came to quiet them. But through those first weeks I would lay in my sleeping place, gazing out at the darkness. There were large trees, and at times Taktik's light would fall on them and the wind would move them. And high in the star-swept gardens of the night, my mind would go back to Nunavut. To my mother and father. Old Siaja. And Tiitaa.

I started those first weeks terribly lonely, often falling asleep with tears in my eyes. Sleeping with the small amulet Siaja had given me clutched in my hand. Waking in the morning with the feelings of a stranger in a strange place.

June 24

Another bad night for Morgan. The fever wouldn't go away, and again he was delirious. I sat by his side until he fell asleep. I was dozing off in the chair when the morning light came through the window. When I lifted my head I realized Morgan was looking at me. Just quietly watching me. I took the damp cloth and pressed it to his lips and he smiled a little.

"I'll be better today," he assured me.

"You should eat something," I said. "I'll make you some food."

"Not now. A little later."

"When you're ready."

"I had a dream," he told me.

"About what?" I asked.

"I was dreaming about Olson and Tiitaa. I don't remember all of it. It was there when I woke but after that I lost it. But I know we were traveling up north again. The three of us. Just like that first trip to Arctic Bay when we wintered with Inuppak's people."

"Was it a good dream?"

"Yes," he said. "I had my health back. And Olson was there. And Tiitaa had that wild, free look in his eyes. You know that look."

"Yes."

"Olson was laughing. I don't remember why. I could hear him in my dream. That part didn't go away."

I wet the cloth and wet his lips again. I pulled the blanket up near his shoulders but he pushed it back. He smiled and said, "I'll be better today. I won't be so hard on you."

Later I went out and filled a pail with clean snow for drinking water. When I came back he was sleeping. But it was a good sleep. A quiet sleep. I think he was traveling with the team and Tiitaa and Olson were there.

June 25

We all had our pictures taken that first month I was at school. Mrs. Colville made a big fuss over it. It was a thing that was done once each year. A man brought in a large box camera and set it up in the big room. Some of the girls knew what was happening and were very excited. I had no idea. It was a Saturday. We were all sent in groups to the laundry room. In the room were large tubs filled with water. And there we were given clean towels and soap and brushes with which to scrub our bodies. We were also given clean underwear, heavy wool stockings, and a long white cotton dress that hung from shoulder to floor and pulled in at the waist with a wide blue band. This was our uniform. And on this day we were marched into the big room and lined in a group under Mrs. Colville's man-agement. Shorter girls in front, taller at the back, and behind us teachers and assistants. Mrs. Col-ville sat in front in a large chair, and we were all forced to hold perfectly still with a fixed smile until the camera went off. I didn't understand what was happening until much later, when I saw the black-and-white photograph.

I eventually made good friends with Celeste LaVeau, a French Canadian. She was two years older than me, tall and slender with brown hair and happy brown eyes. I had been moved into her study group, and her sleeping place was next to mine. She took it upon herself to watch over me. The other girls appeared to listen to Celeste. They respected her.

Celeste first showed her friendship on the day of the photograph. She and I were in the same group sent down for baths and clean clothing. When we had removed our clothes to climb into the tubs, one of the girls saw the amulet Siaja had given me. The ivory snowbird that hung from my neck. And she asked what it was. I told her it was an amulet. A gift from a friend.

She came close and took it in her hand, then let it fall away again. "It's not Christian," she said.

I hesitated. "It has a spirit," I offered.

"But it's not Christian," she said firmly.

Another girl joined in. "It can't have a spirit if it's not Christian."

I told them it had power.

The first laughed and the second joined her, saying it was nothing but silly Eskimo superstition. And again she reached for the amulet. But I caught her hand and pushed it away. She looked surprised and reached out again. This time I caught her arm and pushed much harder, and she stumbled back into the hands of her friend. "You stupid little Eskimo!"

The other girls gathered about. Then Celeste stepped between us. "Leave her alone," she said softly.

"But she pushed me! I almost fell against the tub!"

Celeste said again in the same soft voice, "Leave her alone."

The girl hesitated, looked about at those watching, then backed away. Her friend followed. Then those who had gathered lost interest.

"They're testing you," Celeste told me. "You're new here. And you're different." And she said I shouldn't let it worry me. Then she swung her long legs over the side of the tub and slipped down into the water.

But it did worry me. I was sure I would always have trouble with those girls. But I never did. They never said another unkind word to me.

And Celeste LaVeau became my good friend.

June 26

The man Mrs. Colville called John was slow in some ways. When Mrs. Colville told him to do something, she always told him twice. When she called him, she always called him twice. Some girls teased him. But they never teased him in front of Mrs. Colville.

He was old, his hair silver gray. He was small and thin and walked with bent shoulders, the way old men do. He spoke very little, replying to most things with a simple nod.

He did all kinds of odd jobs around the school. In truth, Mrs. Colville had given him a home there. Probably he could not have stayed as long in another place. He just had too much trouble understanding things. But he worked hard all the time. Fixing and painting, and mostly driving Mrs. Colville about in the automobile or running errands.

When the heavy snows came John put the automobile away. The sleigh came out of the carriage house, and to it he hooked an old horse named Dolly. Dolly was a mournful-looking creature with a slumped back and sad eyes. But once a week John drove her to a small village that lay between the school and Quebec City. One Saturday Mrs. Colville agreed to let Celeste and me join John on the journey. And I think that was when my loneliness started to break.

We were bundled up in heavy buffalo-skin coats and tucked under blankets on the sleigh. Then John snapped the reins easily and said, not in a loud voice, but in a commanding one, "Get on there, girl. Get on, Dolly." And with that Dolly started to move. Slowly at first, then a little faster, with the sleigh lifting slightly and slipping through the snow and with the bells on her neck tinkling in the icy air. "Get on, Dolly."

Dolly trotted at a steady pace, her body steaming in the cold. Along the tree-lined road buried in the snow. Through the dark woods and the mist lifting from the earth. The cold and windblown snow cutting our faces. We followed the river.

Celeste and I huddled close. And later, for a short time, John let Celeste take the reins and drive the sleigh. And then it was my turn, and I drove all the way to the village.

I could smell the wood smoke even before we reached the village, drifting low from the chimneys. And we passed a few little houses, cottages peeking out from a cover of white, and a church. I held tight to the reins, but Dolly was driving herself, now on a road cut from others' sleighs. And on her own she came to a halt at the steps of the general store. But, as if to make it official, John said, "Here, Dolly. Stop, girl." And Celeste and I both laughed.

Celeste told me it was a small store. But to me it held all the things in the world. It was four times the size of the Company store in Foster's Bay. I spent the first minutes simply exploring, with Celeste at my side enjoying my curiosity. And my curiosity was endless. There was food. All kinds of food in cans filling the shelves. And there were pots and knives and cloth. Rolls and rolls of cloth in all colors. A whole rack of dresses. And hats. Hats that ladies wear. And some with ribbons. I tried on a hat, with the ribbon hanging down over my nose. Celeste took me to a long mirror and turned the hat the other way on my head. She laughed. And, putting herself in place of the store owner, offered the hat as her latest fashion from Paris.

I spun in a full circle before the mirror.

"Lovely," she said.

I spun again, almost whirling off my feet and colliding with two women passing by us. As I caught my balance, I heard one say to the other, "I believe that child is Eskimo."

"Eskimo? No?"

"But look at her. The pug nose and flat face."

"But such beautiful dark hair."

"They all have hair like that, Margaret. They wash it in fish oil or something."

I noticed the man behind the counter watching us. Listening to the women. Then his eyes dropped away.

The women passed on with a flow of whispers. Celeste pursed her lips at their passing. Then she found another hat, even more beautiful than the first. I tried it on, and we both filled the store with laughter. The man behind the counter looked up suddenly. "You girls! Leave those things alone!"

Celeste and I fell quiet. Slowly Celeste put the hats back in their place. And then we heard John's seldom-used voice. "They're doing no harm," he said softly.

The man at the counter quickly informed John that he didn't want us handling the merchandise.

We both moved off away from the hats. "I wouldn't buy his dowdy old hats anyway," Celeste said.

The man looked at us angrily. It was certain that he had heard her words. He turned on John. "If they damage something, you'll pay heavily for it." He leaned forward. His voice loud. And then, leering at me, he said, "And I don't want any Indians in my store."

"She's Inuit," John said.

"Same difference."

John turned slowly toward us.

"We'll wait in the sleigh," Celeste offered, and she took my hand. But going out, she turned back once. "Dowdy, frumpy hats."

Celeste and I went out to wait in the sleigh with the patient Dolly. Pulling the heavy blankets over us.

"Stupid man," Celeste whispered. And she said I should pay no attention to anything he said.

I said nothing. Looking back through the frosted windows of the store, I could see old John. He had been confronted by the two women. And the man behind the counter had joined them. I could see them all talking at once and John taking the full weight of it. He stood a little dismayed, searching for words he never used. Not knowing how to turn away. Caught in their ignorance. I felt terrible for him.

When John finally came out he loaded the bundles into the sleigh and untied Dolly from the post. But all the long way back through the blowing snow, he was quiet. He didn't say a single word. And it was a quiet even deeper than his usual silence. And I will always remember that silence. And how I felt so bad for John.

June 27

I took Morgan outside the cabin today and he walked with his weight on my shoulders. When we came back inside he had hot tea. Then we shaved his beard away.

"How do I look?" he asked me

"You look better," I said.

"I feel stronger," he told me. Then he was quiet. I think he wanted me to reassure him. But in truth he was pale and gaunt and his eyes hollow.

"Did you have another dream?" I asked him, wanting to break the silence.

He looked at me questioningly.

"The other night you were dreaming about Olson, and Tiitaa," I told him. "And you were traveling up north again."

He shook his head. "I don't remember."

"You said it was a good dream."

He was thoughtful. "I don't like to forget good dreams," he said. "I should have kept that one."

"Dreams aren't like memories," I told him. "They are smoky things. We can't keep them."

"Yes. that's true. But a little unfair." He laid down again and turned toward me. "Right now good dreams are all I have. I can't afford to lose what little I have."

"That will change," I told him. "When the *Venture* comes it will all change."

He smiled. "My optimistic Maata," he said. "You dream enough for both of us."

June 28

My education took wing during the two years I spent at Mrs. Colville's. We had only four hours of learning time each day, plus the study time each evening. But those hours were packed solidly.

The school was self-reliant in many ways. The girls who went there were not privileged. We worked hard. Each of us was assigned some task, and that task changed each month. It may be working in the gardens in the spring or summer. Or working in the kitchen or laundry. Or even cutting firewood. Or cleaning the stable or carriage house. Polishing the brass lamps or scrubbing the floor in the big room. We all had our turn. The tuition was small. Mine was covered by Reverend Moorehead, but others could afford it even less. So it was not unusual to find Mrs. Colville in the kitchen bending over steaming pots of soup or stew, or hours later bending over a washboard in the laundry, or teaching a class in history or grammar. She was what she expected her girls to be, or to become. And in every way the school reflected her personality.

Off the big room was the library. Shelves of big books and little books. Some out in the open so you could touch them. Others behind glass, protected like sacred things. Siaja said that books have spirits, and I think when I entered this room I could feel them all about me. It was my favorite place in the whole school. And the best months were those when I was assigned to that room, to dust the books and the shelves, clean the glass, and polish the dark wood.

My second favorite place was in the gardens. I did not know food could be grown from the earth in such a way. In Nunavut we gathered a few berries in late summer or early autumn. But because of the permafrost, we grew nothing of our own on the tundra. Here things sprouted from the earth. I could see them growing. We had three gardens. One for herbs, one for vegetables, and one for flowers. To keep out rabbits and deer, a stone wall surrounded the herb and vegetable gardens. But the wall was no higher than my head. I told old John that a caribou could easily jump over it. "So could one of our deer," said John. "But a deer will never jump over something if he doesn't know what's on the far side."

That was the longest conversation John ever held with me. Except for one other time, when he showed me how to set in poles for the beans to climb.

Celeste said I was becoming "a little Eskimo farmer." And she laughed at my dirty hands and dirty face. But I loved the smell of the dirt. The rich smell of the earth.

That first spring and summer were plentiful. And by mid-autumn we put up enough jars of fruits and vegetables to fill all the shelves in the pantry, and then some. Still the orchards were heavy with fruit, and there were bushels of corn left over. John hooked old Dolly up to a flat wagon and made another trip into the village with the extra produce, and there he traded for rolls of cloth that the girls cut and sewed into new uniforms. I helped with the hand sewing while a few used machines, and Mrs. Colville remarked that she had never seen a girl make stitches so close and so tight. I told her my mother had taught me when I helped to sew our winter clothes.

Mrs. Colville asked if my mother had taught me English. I said Siaja had taught me the Qallunaat words.

She was thoughtful a moment. "And am I Qallunaat?"

"Qallunaaq," I told her. "Singular."

"I see. Well, I guess that's fine. And who taught you to read and write so well?" I gave credit to Mr. Sanders and the little school in Foster's Bay. And Mr. Webster's big book. She nodded. Then she rested her hand firmly on my shoulder. "You are a fortunate girl, Sarah."

"Maata," I said, but smiled as I said it.

She smiled. Then went away.

The winter snows in Quebec came fast and deep. I think it snowed more in Quebec than it did in my north country. But it was a wet snow and not good for much of anything, except being snow. But still it was beautiful. And on our free Sunday time Celeste and I would take long walks. Celeste was not very good at breaking snow trails, so I always went first. Celeste wanted to walk along the road or in places where the snow had been cleared by the wind. But I enjoyed walking deep in the woods because snow with trees was a new thing to me. After little time Celeste would have a red nose and red cheeks from the cold. She would start complaining. She got cold easily. But I would try to go as far as I could go.

Once, as we neared a small clearing, we heard a loud commotion. In the center of the clearing was a fallen tree, and the noise was coming from the other side of it. I heard it first and stopped. Celeste came up to me. "What is it?" She spoke in a whisper. I shook my head. I didn't know.

We waited, listening. Then we could see the branches of the tree shaking, the snow falling free of them. At times shaking frantically. Then stopping.

I moved out into the clearing, making my way around the fallen tree. The shaking started again, and I stopped and waited. When all was quiet I moved up slowly. Once I looked back at Celeste. She had taken cover behind a bush and was peering out at me. I moved on. But I knew I was making far too much noise with my boots crushing the snow. The creature there had to know I was coming. Then, as I rounded the fallen branches, I saw the gray body of an animal. I moved closer to get a better look. Then I called to Celeste to come out of hiding. But she wouldn't move without knowing what it was.

"A deer," I called back.

She demanded to know what it was doing.

It had its antlers caught in the branches of the fallen tree and couldn't get free. I called out and waited.

Cautiously Celeste made her way to me. "Oh! Look at it!"

It was a young male deer, and I could see the panic in his eyes. He had been trying frantically to free himself but had only worked in tighter. He must have heard us coming through the woods, and that terrorized him even more.

Celeste was full of questions. How did he get caught like that? What was he doing there?

Probably trying to strip the bark away for food, I told her. He worked his antlers in between the branches and got caught.

"I didn't know deer ate trees."

"They are eating bark because they can't find grass in the deep snow."

Celeste thought about it. "But what are we going to do?"

"If I had a knife or something, I could kill it," I said.

Celeste looked at me in horror.

"It's meat," I told her. And I looked around us, but all the ground was snow covered. I told her to search for a rock or something sharp.

"No!" Her refusal was absolute.

"Then you stay here and make sure it doesn't get away. I'll run back to the kitchen and get a knife." But her refusal was just as firm. She would have no part of it.

The deer pulled wildly at the branches, twisting its head in an effort to get loose. Celeste looked at me. She was almost as frantic as the deer. Then she accused me of scaring the animal.

"Well?" I asked. "What do you want to do?"

First she looked puzzled. Then a moment later

she suggested that we should just go away as though we had never found it.

"It will starve to death if it doesn't get free," I said.

She thought more about it. "Then we have to free it."

"Free it? How?"

"I don't know. You're the Eskimo. You know all about animals."

I shook my head. "We don't free them."

"Look at the poor thing," Celeste said. And she went on and on, pleading with me, comforting the deer. Going almost into tears. "Please, Maata?" Until finally I agreed.

I climbed up into the branches as Celeste watched. The deer was strangely calm. Almost as though he had accepted the worst. I worked my way in past the antlers to a large branch where I could balance myself. The deer waited, breathing heavily through his nostrils, his brown eyes glazed in fright. I came to the branch that was locking him in, a thick branch caught just behind his rack. I tried to push it free with my boot. It moved but not far enough. The deer must have felt the difference because he started to pull. But the branch was too much. I called to Celeste to pull on the end of it.

With both hands Celeste pulled until the branch started to bow. I put the weight of both boots on it, pushing as hard as I could. The deer pulled, then suddenly he was free. He went back on shaky legs, falling into the snow. The branch whipped back, taking Celeste with it. And Celeste went into the snow. The deer was up and bounding off into the woods before she was on her feet. She was laughing. "Look at him run, Maata!"

The deer ran to the edge of the trees, just into the gray shadows, then he stopped and turned toward us. He lingered there only a few seconds. Then he turned to leap away.

"He's gone," she said. She sounded a little disappointed.

I sat back on a heavy branch and looked at her. "You wanted him to be free."

"Yes. But I hoped he would stay for a little while," she said. She was happy and frowning at the same time.

June 29

I think Morgan heard it at the same time I did. I was walking down by the sea edge, and Morgan was back in the cabin. And when I heard it I went running back to him. Running up the rocky slope with my heart pounding. I threw open the cabin door shouting, "Morgan! Morgan!" But he already had the field glasses at the window.

It was the *Venture*. She was moving north.

I joined him at the window just as the whistle sounded again, long and lonely over the dark sea. He passed me the field glasses, and I adjusted them to my eyes. She was out a great distance, but I could see her gray shape on the horizon and the black smoke from her stacks. Going up north to the settlements before she turned south again.

I watched silently, for a long time, until she faded over the curve of the earth. Then I lowered the glasses. "She'll be back," I said.

"Yes," he told me. "Yes. Of course."

"She'll be back," I said again.

July 2

Celeste said that I dreamed a lot at night and that at times I tossed and cried in my sleep. One night I must have had a bad dream because she woke me so I wouldn't bother the other girls.

I think I was dreaming about my mother and father and the boat and the ice. When I woke I was shaking, and Celeste wrapped the blanket around me. "I want to go home," I whispered.

"You are home," she told me.

I told her I wanted to go north. To my home.

"Isn't it better here?" she asked.

"I do not belong here," I told her.

"But this is where we are now," said Celeste. And she said we had to make the best of it.

I was quiet. Pulling the blanket tight about my shoulders. Looking off for a moment at the night sky beyond the window. Then I asked her if she didn't want to go home.

She shook her head. "I have no home," she said. "My mother died when I was born."

She had never spoken of it before. She told me her father didn't want to keep her after her mother was gone. For several years she lived with an aunt. But the woman was old. And before the aunt died she made arrangements for Celeste to come to Mrs. Colville's.

"But you can't spend the rest of your life here."

"I won't," she said. And she told me her dream. To marry a very handsome man. A rich man. And live like a lady.

"Like the ladies in the village?"

"Like that. But not like them."

And she would have a big house and many children. And her children would all go to universities to be doctors and lawyers.

"And I will come and visit you."

"Yes. Definitely," she said.

"And you can visit me."

"No. Never," she said, knowing that she would never travel that far north.

I told her I would have a little house. A house cut with a snow knife. And my sons would be great hunters and sing the songs hunters sing. The songs of my father.

We talked and shared our dreams. Knowing we were so very different. And yet the same. And she raised her hand to mine and we locked them tightly. Our spirits locking together. Promising always to be friends.

July 5

One day, in early summer, Celeste came running into the garden where I was working with John. She was all excited, with a big smile on her face. There was a stranger in the library with Mrs. Colville!

According to Celeste, he was the most handsome man in the world. "Come on, Maata!" She took hold of my hand and started pulling me.

"Slow down," I told her.

"No. You've got to see."

"Is it your rich husband?"

"Oh! Don't I wish!"

As we neared the big room, Celeste put her finger to her lips for quiet. "We'll wait here across from the door," she said. "And when they come out you'll—"

Mrs. Colville's voice cut Celeste short. "Well! There she is now."

I turned to see my Olson standing beside Mrs. Colville, almost dwarfing her with his size. There was a big grin on his face. "You ready to go home?" he asked, as if it were nothing.

I made a run and one leap, and he swung me into the air in a full circle. And I remember shouting his name over and over again. Olson! Olson!

He laughed. I had tears in my eyes.

Mrs. Colville was laughing. Celeste was stunned into complete silence.

"Did you think we would simply forget you?" Olson asked as my feet hit the floor.

"I thought I would never see home again," I told him.

"Well," said Olson. "You were wrong. And you'd better start packing. We have a boat to catch. The *Venture*. And she's sailing tonight."

Wiping the tears from my eyes, I looked to Mrs. Colville. She held up a letter she had been holding. A letter signed by Reverend Moorehead. I could return north with Olson or I could stay at the school. He said the choice should be left to me.

"Well?" Olson asked. "Are you packing?"

It wasn't even a question in my mind. And Olson knew by the look in my eyes. I nodded, still wiping tears away.

Daniel Morgan was already in Foster's Bay, he told me. They had learned where I was from Reverend Moorehead. Morgan was putting together a good dog team. They wanted to start for Igloolik with the first snow of autumn. We would winter with Tiitaa and his people.

I remembered Celeste and ran to her. She was weeping. The tears streaming down her face. I didn't want to leave her.

Between sobs she told me I had to go. I had to

go to be happy. We held each other close for a long moment. "I'll help you pack your things," she told me. "But I'll cry all the time we are doing it."

Then our hands locked, our spirits locking together.

chapter seven

~ July 6, 1924 ~

We left Foster's Bay with the first good snow that covered the ground. And we ran with all the daylight hours. My heart swelled with the immensity of my land. Of the sky against the earth. Of the cold, clean air biting my face. Of the sound of the sled and the snap of Morgan's whip. I was living again freely. And in my own world.

After two days north we ran on the sea ice. We saw polar bear and white fox and seal. On the fourth day Morgan shot a seal near its breathing hole. Olson and I butchered it out. Extra meat for

PAUL SULLIVAN

ourselves and the dogs. Olson made a disgusting face as I ate the meat raw steaming in the cold. Sitting on the ice and enjoying every sweet moment of it. "All of that education and you're still a savage," he said.

Morgan laughed. That good laugh that made me feel at home again. He told Olson they could never take the wild out of an Inuit. And probably shouldn't try.

I reminded Olson that at Mrs. Colville's we had no such delicacies.

He shook his head with a laugh and walked away.

We left the sea ice for a rolling land of snow-covered hills and valleys. We saw a small herd of caribou and later a place where wolves made a kill. One day a raven swept down to follow us for a long time. The raven, who my father had said brought light to the world, I believed was welcoming me home. His wings laying a shadow on the snow.

Each day we ran until darkness fell, then Morgan and I would take the dogs from harness while Olson put the tent up and started the little stove. And each night before sleeping I would walk out into the darkness to thank Taktik for watching over me. For I knew he had followed me south to ease my heart. And clutching Siaja's amulet, I would look up at the stars so large and so bright. And I spoke to Siaja beyond the star-swept gardens of the night. And I told her of all the spirits of all the books. As many as there are Inuit. And as many words as there are stars. And I told my father how my friend Celeste and I freed the deer. And I told Mother how I missed her warmth. And when I went to my sleeping place, there were no tears in my eyes. I was happy. I listened to the wind soft against the tent. And slept contented.

When you have known a faraway place, you truly know your own. How important the people are. How special the land is. For when you return you see with different eyes and measure with a different heart.

Even then I understood that I owed much to Reverend Moorehead for sending me away. I owed Mrs. Colville for caring for me. And Celeste for loving me as a friend. If not for them, for their doing, for what they gave, I would not fully know today what I have.

I am Inuk. Of the Inuit people. A child of Nunavut.

✳

July 7

The settlement of Igloolik was as Tiitaa described it. It was a place of many houses huddled tightly against the frozen sea.

We spent several days there, picking up supplies and resting the dogs. Olson wrote a long letter to his wife and left it with the manager of the Bay Company store for the next supply ship. Morgan told Olson, "That woman must surely love you to put up with all the drifting you do."

Olson said he was going to settle down when this trip was over. Go home and raise a family.

"You said the same thing before they shipped you to France," Morgan reminded him.

Tiitaa had left word at the Company Store that his people would set up their winter camp south of Arctic Bay. Morgan and Olson knew the place having been there before. So on a bright morning we crossed the ice that covered Fox Basin. And the next day we were on Baffin Island, with the dogs running well on the hard snow.

The dogs were running well, but Morgan didn't appear eager to push them. I knew we could make much better time with a little more effort from the team and the sound of Morgan's whip. I was eager to see Tiitaa and Inuppak again. But Morgan was content with making the journey last. We camped earlier those last days, wasting much of the light from Hekenjuk. But I said nothing. Then one evening Olson said to me, "Morgan is coming back too. Back from the war. In a way we're all coming back. You, Daniel Morgan, and myself."

I told Olson I knew very little about the war.

"There's not a lot you need to know," he told me. "Only that it was a horrible thing. And a terrible waste of life."

"And why did it happen?"

Olson thought for a moment. "Old men lied. Young men believed them."

He said nothing after that. But I could tell the war was still with him. And with Morgan. It was written in their eyes. And their laughter was still touched with it. And I realized that for some reason, the solitude of the tundra seemed to help it.

When we came across a herd of caribou in a narrow valley, Morgan killed two at a great distance with his rifle. We butchered them there, and as the meat froze in the cold, we loaded it on the sled and covered it with the hides. Morgan said it would be extra meat for Tiitaa and his people.

But with the weight, I knew the team would

travel even slower. And with the extra weight much time was spent helping the team move the heavy *kamotik* up steep slopes or through deep snow. Or slowing the team on an icy grade.

Going down one very sharp incline, the sled got away from us. It gained speed by its own weight and overran the dogs, catching their traces under the *kamotik* and plowing into them. One dog was killed and a second suffered a broken leg. The *kamotik* ended on its side against a wall of ice but was not damaged. Morgan shot the second dog as I butchered out the first. Then I butchered out the second. It was food for the remaining six.

We were traveling slowly. The six dogs now taking all the weight of the *kamotik*. And the three of us walked with the team. The distance we could have covered with a running team in a day took two or more days. And the wind came up angrily, blowing icy snow over the surface of the land. But none of us spoke of dumping the meat tied to the *kamotik*. We knew too well how important it would be if the caches ran low during the winter.

It was another two weeks of hard travel on foot before we neared Arctic Bay. And during that time we were hit twice with brutal storms that tore across the land, building heavy drifts. It was too much for the tent, so we built a snow house while outside the six dogs dug in using the snow for a blanket. After the passing of each storm the day was clear and bright again but the going far more difficult with the new snow. Finally, when Morgan knew we could be no more than a single day's travel by dog team from Tiitaa's winter camp, we made a cache to store away the meat, covering it with hides and heavy rocks. We made camp there that night, ready to finish the journey the next morning. But I slept little, being so anxious to see Tiitaa and Inuppak again.

I was awake, just as dawn was coming, when I heard the commotion outside. Our team barking and snarling. Morgan was first out with this rifle, with Olson and I following. In the distance we saw what caught the team's attention. Three heavy *kamotiks,* each pulled by a line of fine huskies, coming fast in our direction. Down the long slope of a hill and across the windblown snow. Hunters returning to camp. The first team reached us and came to a stop. Then the second and third halted nearby. It was easy to see that they had been running hard, with the dogs panting and ice clinging to the parkas of the men. Then one imposing hunter secured his whip to the sled, turned slowly toward me, and smiled. His beard and the hood of his parka were so heavy with ice, I did not recognize him. But when he laughed I knew it was Tiitaa. He took another step closer and was crushing me in his arms as if he were a big, happy bear. "Little sister is home," he said, and he said it again and again.

"Oh, Tiitaa! Father and Mother are gone."

"I know," he told me. "Their spirits are gone. But your spirit is here. Little sister is home."

July 8

Inuppak was with child. She said the birth would come soon, before Hekenjuk went away south again. She was even more beautiful. Perhaps because of the child in her body. There was a radiance about her, something from joy. "I am so pleased you are here," she said. "Here to share this with me." She took my hand in hers and placed it on her swollen stomach to feel the life inside.

I waited, her hand pressing mine on her belly, then I felt a little kick. I looked at Inuppak with my eyes wide.

"The old women say I carry this child as if it were a boy," she said proudly. "The old women know things."

I felt the little kick again, against the palm of my hand, and I laughed. Pleased for her and Tiitaa. And happy for myself for being with them.

The winter camp was on a slope of ground above the sea ice. The place had been used many times before because the hunting had always been good there. I heard a hunter tell Olson that in the spring the little white whales, the belugas, often came in close to the shore. This did not happen each year, but it happened on occasion. When it did it was a most exciting thing for the people.

But the autumn hunting this year had been poor. The caribou had passed very far to the south and not in the great numbers. Though there was meat in the caches, they were not full, and a long hard winter could bring hunger. So after we were in camp only a few hours, Morgan, Olson, and Tiitaa went out with a group of hunters to retrieve the cache we had stored on the tundra. They hoped to find the feeding herds we had passed on our journey up from Igloolik. The hunters took five teams of dogs and enough food to last a week.

The cold had come early to the north of Baffin Island. The sea ice was solid with long walls of barrier ice, that ice piled near the shore by winds and tides, separating the sea from the camp. The snow was deep and hard. It was *pokanaqyuk,* snow good for building, and the little village of snow houses climbed away from the sea. In the center was a common house, built big enough to hold a large group of people. And outside the village was the place where the dogs were kept.

The week the men were away most of the women gathered in the common house to sew winter clothes, watch the children, and tell stories. They all came to enjoy the stories I told, of the ways of the Qallunaat in the far south, and forced me again and again to tell them of Celeste and the deer. Each time I told the story and the deer ran free, they laughed with amazement. But some voiced their dismay. "How will these people eat?" a woman questioned.

I explained that they grow things. From the earth. "And they have chickens and cows."

She looked at me skeptically. "Grow things? In the frozen earth?"

"The earth is not frozen in that place," I said.

"It is not tundra?"

"No."

The old woman shook her head.

"Not a good place to live," said another.

"It is different," I told them, and hoped they

would ask no more questions. But after a short time one would ask that I repeat a story from before. Then it would start all over again. And, at one point, when I told them that often the women there do not sew things as we do but use a machine, the explaining became impossible. I think that even Inuppak thought I might be imagining. I had thought of telling them of John and the automobile and the old horse, Dolly. But I decided against it.

Often I just wanted to be alone. I was so happy to be home again that I just wanted to be with the land. I took long walks on the snow-covered tundra. Listening to the wind. Watching the clouds in the sky. Following the tracks of a fox or watching a snowbird fly. At times they were the very best moments.

When the men returned from the hunt, there was enough meat to fill the caches and enough hides to keep the women working through the winter. The women prepared a feast, and that night in the common house there was storytelling and dancing to the drum.

Tiitaa was the last to dance to the drum, and I saw that Father had taught him well. When Tiitaa put words to the drum, all fell quiet. There was a hush and hearts were listening. I was very proud of Tiitaa. When I looked at Inuppak there was pride in her eyes.

When it came time for Inuppak to give birth, she invited me to stay with her. Tiitaa was sent away, taken by Morgan and Olson and some of the hunters to hunt seal on the ice. Tiitaa protested, saying the ice was too thick and there were no breathing holes to be found. But still they took him away.

Three women came into the snow house to help with the birth. Inuppak, as is the custom with Inuit women, crouched on a caribou skin. We held her hands. Another sat at her back to hug her stomach and help with the birth. An old woman, who had delivered many babies, waited to receive this newborn.

Inuppak was a long time in labor. Her moans of pain became cries of agony. Her beautiful face drew up tight, and tears came from her eyes. Her teeth pressed deep into her bottom lip. Each contraction took her breath away. I looked at the old woman waiting calmly between her legs. But I was frightened for Inuppak. And then the old woman smiled. Inuppak screamed. A long scream, throwing her head back and her long hair streaming down. She screamed with her mouth fixed open and her eyes bulging. It was horrible. The old woman smiled and laughed again. Then she pulled the newborn free. Inuppak fell back into the arms of the one holding her. For a second her eyes closed. Then there was a little cry. The first sound of new life. Inuppak opened her eyes. The old woman held the newborn up for the mother to see.

The old woman laughed. "A son," she said. And she turned the child so Inuppak could see his penis.

We all laughed. Inuppak laughed with us, even though she was crying.

The old woman quickly tied the umbilical cord and then she cut it away. The newborn was wiped down, and one of the women took the placenta out of the snow house. Then the child was laid in Inuppak's arms against her breast. Gently she ran her fingers over his tiny face. Then over his arms and his small hands and fingers. Over his legs and his toes.

The old woman whispered, "He is good, Inuppak. He will be a hunter. One to bring joy when you are young. One to bring food when you are old."

But I believe Inuppak did not hear a word the old woman said. She was listening to the breathing of her son.

I went down to the sea ice where the men were waiting. From one of the ice ridges, I called out to Tiitaa. "My brother! You are a father now!"

Tiitaa came away from the group of men. He held his hand to his ear as if he hadn't heard my words.

I called out again. "It is a boy child! Inuppak and the child are waiting for you!"

He heard my words the second time, for he came running over the ice. When he had almost neared the place where I stood, his feet went out from under him, his legs in the air, and he fell, sliding across the ice. The men started laughing at him. But Tiitaa paid them no attention. He was up and running again. Almost running even before he was up.

"A boy," I told him as he reached me. "A little hunter. And Inuppak is well and waiting for you." But if he heard my words this time, he never slowed or showed any sign of hearing. He hurried on, up the hard snow path to the camp.

They gave this child the name of Otek. The name of Inuppak's grandfather, who had long ago died on the ice. So the spirit of the grandfather lived in the newborn. He was small and chubby with a thick crop of black hair. When he wasn't crying he was laughing. And when he wasn't sleeping his baby hands reached out for all things. He became fond of my hair and liked to tangle it in his fingers or put it in his mouth. And he liked to catch the amulet that hung from my neck. Inuppak often allowed me to carry little Otek in my *amoutik*, my woman's parka, around the camp. And though there were a number of children in the camp, it was evident to me that none were as handsome as my nephew.

The Inuit have no names for months, as the Qallunaat do. Our year is simply divided into seasons. Autumn, when the slush ice appears on the water and the first snows come. Winter, when Taktik is long in the sky. Spring, when Hekenjuk comes home from the south. And summer, when the ice is gone. And there are few words in our language for *good-bye*. It is seldom said, or needed. Morgan and Olson stayed with us at the winter camp until early spring. Then they decided to start south while the snow was still good for the dogs to travel on. And though I had learned a hundred ways to say good-bye in the English language, I did it with great difficulty. My eyes were wet with tears the morning they made ready to leave. My good friends, whom I had come to love as brothers. Part of my new family. My heart was also a little restless to journey with them. For I had seen some of the world, and that had whet my curiosity. But at the same time my heart wanted to stay with Tiitaa and his people.

Daniel Morgan promised they'd be back.

And Olson said, "You keep safe, little one."

All the people of the camp gathered to watch them leave. And the children ran with their sled a long distance, until they could not keep pace with the dogs. Then they reached the white horizon and crossed over it. And I felt a little empty when they were gone.

July 10

I watch for the *Venture* moving south again. Each morning now I take the field glasses and go up to the high ground, and there I search the sea, hoping to find the ship. There is no ice now, just the blue gray sea. Under a clear sky I can see for a great distance.

There are new flowers on the tundra. Thick

Arctic heather clings to the rocks. The hills are laced with buttercups and cotton grass. I made a band of flowers for Morgan's big floppy hat. Like a bonnet now.

On this morning I put flowers on Olson's grave, as I had promised him.

I have seen no bears for many days. But I have seen foxes drifting back and forth over the hills. Their short legs hurrying away to search for birds' eggs or lemmings. But I have found no birds' eggs. I have seen a pair of hawks nesting in the cliff near the sea.

I searched the rocky beach for driftwood and gathered two small bundles. Each day I find some that the sea has given up, some not there from before.

Today, when I sat on the rocks and watched the sea lap over the stony beach, I thought about my father. Father and his boat. And in my mind I could see him skipping over the surface of the water, listening to the engine, and saying as he would, "A fine thing. A fine thing for a man to have." And that happy smile on his face. Laughing. I asked Father if he had seen the *Venture* returning, or even the *North Wind*. And, if his spirit were passing, to hurry them to Tumak.

My heart was asking, for I believe Morgan has few days left now.

I brought flowers to the cabin and fixed them in a tin cup on the table. Morgan did not notice.

When I swung the field glasses and the rifle from my shoulder, he asked what I had seen. I told him about the fox and the hawks on the cliff and the driftwood I had gathered.

"On the horizon?" he asked. "No smoke? No ship?"

I shook my head and turned slowly away from him. Arranging the flowers. Hanging the big floppy hat on a wall peg. When I turned back he looked away from me.

I told him the weather had been good. No bad seas. That the *Venture* could be back this way very soon now. Maybe even tomorrow.

He was silent, with that doubtful silence that comes over him. Drawing him away.

I offered to cut his hair again. And shave the beard from his face. And heat some water for washing.

"Yes. I should make a good appearance," he said. But his voice showed his lack of interest.

"Would you like to go out in the sun? The sun is good for you."

"Not now, Maata."

"I'll make tea. There is a little tea I've been saving. And we have a few biscuits."

"I couldn't chew the biscuits."

"You can soak them in the tea."

"Yes." He looked at me. His eyes deep in his face and a glazed look. His voice changed as he said, "I don't have any family to worry about. Just a sister outside of Boston. But, of course, she should know." And then he went on in that same voice, telling me I should write to Olson's wife. He wouldn't tell me what to say. I was far better with words on paper. But I should do that.

I pulled the lid from the biscuit tin. There were three biscuits left.

"Are you listening?"

"No. I am not listening."

He ignored me and started on again. A little annoyed. Telling me he needed to know I would do those things.

"I will do as you ask," I told him. "But now I am not listening." I broke one biscuit in half and put half back in the tin.

He fell quiet. He sat in the window light and looked out at the sea for a moment. Then he turned to me. "Will you help me up to Olson's grave? I know it will be difficult."

"Yes. We will go tomorrow," I told him. I put a piece of wood in the little iron stove to start the tea. I poured water from the bucket into a pot to warm on the stove. Then I put out the scissors and the razor. I took a little water for the flowers in the tin cup and placed them on the table where the light came through the window.

Morgan was again looking out the window and far away.

July 11

Twice we fell on the rocks. After only a short distance Morgan would be forced to stop and rest. But this morning I got Morgan up to the place where Olson is buried. And Morgan sat for a time with his friend.

I left him there. But I didn't go far away. Then I returned later, when the wind was coming up off the sea. I lowered the rifle from my shoulder and sat beside him. It was lonely and sad but strangely nice sitting there. For a long, long time we said nothing. The wind bent the cotton grass below the hill, and one of the nesting hawks hunted above the cliffs. The sea was gray and brooding. The sky silver blue.

He talked about Olson. How Olson said he was going home after this trip. Going home to stay. But, of course, Olson said that after every trip.

Morgan told me, "The trouble with men like Olson is, they're not sure where the end of the world really is. It's as if they've got to find it before they can really go home again."

"But you are going home," I said.

He laughed slightly.

"I know," I said. And I told him how I asked my father to have his spirit find the *Venture* and send her to us. "Father is a great hunter. He will find the *Venture*."

He looked at me. The laughter was still on his face. But he kept the laughter to himself. "Keep believing," he said. "Believe for both of us."

"It will be," I told him. "I know it will be."

"Keep believing," he said again.

July 12

When spring came Tiitaa's people did not move away from their winter camp. They stayed by the sea. Before the good snow went away Tiitaa and some hunters made a trading run to Igloolik. And

Tiitaa brought back the first sugar candy for little Otek. I laughed at the expression on his round face as he popped it in his mouth, then reached for more. We all laughed at his puzzlement, and then at his pleasure.

Tiitaa said the sugar candy was all of the Qallunaat way of life that his son would ever know. I knew that Tiitaa was wrong. For I had been south and knew that the Qallunaat were so many that in the coming years he could not avoid them. But I did not argue with my brother. Tiitaa was happy in his world, and I would not spoil it.

The cry of the wolf. The flight of the raven. The wind on the snow. All special things. But none as special as the song of the whales. The little white whales. The belugas. And one night in late spring I woke to the song of the whales. All in the camp woke and gathered at the water's edge. And in the golden light that Taktik dropped on the dark water, we saw the pod passing. Their white bodies lifting to cut the surface. Their squeaking and chortling, like a celebration. One after another, side by side, twos and threes passing. And we stood as silent as the night watching. All of the camp gathered there. Not a word was spoken as we listened to the language of the whales. Telling of night and the sea. Of life beyond our knowing. I stood in empathy. Their cries carrying my spirit over the moon-swept ocean.

We would kill them if we could reach them. Their oil would light our lamps. Their meat fill our bellies. But in the darkness no boats were launched from the shore. We watched them in passing. And I was not unhappy. A little like Celeste, my heart rejoiced at their going. Strange, but I said nothing to the others.

At dawn the hunters went out but found nothing on the open ocean. And though we lingered at the camp until early summer, the whales did not pass again.

We moved to a new camp. A place below high cliffs where the women could gather birds' eggs. And a place where the fishing was good. A place new to me but used, Tiitaa said, by the ancient ones. We moved into tents for the short weeks of summer. And Inuppak and I took Otek exploring over the summer tundra, gathering moss and Arctic willow and, much later, berries. From a place high on the cliffs, we could look down on the little summer camp. The tents and the smoke lifting away from the fires. Much like the last camp I had known with my father and mother before we were forced off to Foster's Bay almost ten years before.

Inuppak told me she was born at this camp. Out there on the water her grandfather lost his life when he went through the ice. Her mother and father had graves in the shadow of the hill. "This is my summer home," she whispered. "My place." And she said Otek would know this camp. And his children would know it. "This Tiitaa has promised me."

"My brother is Inutuinnait," I said. "A true Inuk. But it may not always be as he promised."

Inuppak caught me with the softness of her eyes. "If things are good, it will be for the time of our life," she said. And there was knowledge in her voice that I had not known before.

I hesitated, then offered, "It would be good for little Otek to know the Qallunaat language. When he starts to form words I will teach him. I will teach him if Tiitaa agrees and it pleases you."

Inuppak fell quiet for a long moment, and then she said, "I will talk to Tiitaa." But I heard a reluctance in her voice that I had never heard before.

I did not realize fully what I had done. Several days later I would know. I was sitting in the grass with little Otek. We were playing with a litter of husky pups when Tiitaa came storming out of the tent. He reached down and swept the child up in his arms and looked at me with rage in his eyes. His face was hard and brooding. "You will not speak Qallunaat words to this child! He is Inuk! The language of his people will be his language!" And he never gave me a chance to reply but went off with little Otek in his arms.

Inuppak came out a moment later. "I am sorry," she said. "I did not know he would have such anger at this thing."

And after that things changed for me with my brother. I was given less time with little Otek. Tiitaa was like an animal protecting his young. I was made distant. It was never spoken of, but I felt it. Even Inuppak was more guarded. Perhaps because Tiitaa wished it. And Inuppak followed the wishes of her husband. It hurt my heart deeply.

In the time that followed I was much more careful in expressing my thoughts. When the women gathered I never told stories of my time in the south. If I told stories, they were of the time before Foster's Bay. And I was careful when using my own language not to break into English words.

A habit that I had fallen into when learning the language with Siaja. But more and more I realized that because I had lived with the whites in the south, Tiitaa would always be wary of me. He loved me and protected me as a sister, but he did not trust what I had learned.

With the first snows we moved back to the winter camp. After only a few days at the winter camp, the hunters went out on long trips to hunt the caribou, to fill the caches with meat. The hunting was good and the caches filled in a short time. As in the past, the women prepared a feast, and there was dancing and singing to the sound of the drum. Again it was Tiitaa who drew the greatest admiration when he danced to Father's old songs. I watched as his body swung low on bent knees and the drum turned in his hand.

Keewatin? North Wind?
Carry my words over the silent stones and blue ice.
Lift the wings of the raven who brought light to the world.
For in his flight the shadow of his wings sweeps over the ancient bones.

And tell them it is the same
land without change.
And the same we will leave
for those who follow.
The tundra and the sea, Nunavut.

I saw the pride in Inuppak's eyes. I saw the warm glow on the faces of the people. They were gathered in song at the edge of the world. At that place where morning starts yet darkness goes unbroken. And they were happy.

I watched little Otek and wanted to reach for him. But I sat silently beyond the circle.

chapter eight

Morgan took the shotgun while I was sleeping. The box of shells was open on the table. The gun lay on Morgan's sleeping place by his side. I looked at him questioningly. He must have read the worry on my face because he hesitated, then told me, "The bear was back last night."

"I didn't hear him," I said.

"No. And I didn't wake you. There was no reason to wake you." He said the bear was just hanging about the cabin. But he knew he was there.

I reached for the gun, but Morgan laid his hand

on it. I offered to put it away, but Morgan said to leave it. His voice almost demanding. His hand was yellow and trembling on the dark stock of the gun. His fingers trying to take hold. "What is it? Don't you trust me, Maata?"

I didn't answer, though I knew he was waiting for a reply. I couldn't answer yes or no honestly. My heart was not sure. Finally I told him I didn't think the bear would be back. It was all I could offer.

Morgan drew the gun up over his legs. With weak hands he opened the chambers. Then he pulled a shell from each chamber and held them up for me to see. "Two," he said. "For the bear. Not me. Strange. I never really thought about it." And he asked if a man would load two shells in a shotgun to use the gun on himself. Two shells in a shotgun, knowing what one can do to a person. His eyes fixed on me as if I should answer his question.

I pressed my lips. I gave the only answer I could. I didn't know.

"Yes. And I don't know either," he said. "Not having seriously thought about it. I've been thinking about a lot of things. Life. Dying. The things I've done and the things I've never done. I've spent some time here feeling sorry for myself and some being grateful. But not much time thinking about one chamber or two chambers."

I fell quiet. Then I said, "If the bear comes back, you should wake me."

"I will wake you."

"I will be uncomfortable if you tell me later and didn't wake me."

He promised me. Then he handed me the two shells. And then the shotgun.

Late this morning I walked around the cabin. Up on the high ground and down near the water. But I saw no signs of the bear.

July 15

Siaja taught me my first words in English. I learned to love words and what I could do with them. At times words flow in my head in special ways, and I want to put them on paper. It is a way of seeing with the mind. I wanted to share this with little Otek. The way my father shared his drum songs with others. But Tiitaa did not understand.

When spring came Morgan and Olson returned to Tiitaa's winter camp. And seeing them was the first real joy I felt in months. They came up from Igloolik. Big Olson with a bag of sugar candy. "Some for Otek," he said. "And some for the little Eskimo girl." And he filled my hand with the sweet candy. But Morgan reminded him that I was not such a little girl any longer. And it was true that I had grown much over the winter. I told Olson that I would be sixteen years very soon.

Olson picked up little Otek and swung him high into the air. I don't think Otek had ever been so high. "And this one. Look how he's grown."

I could see the pleasure in Inuppak's smile. For Inuppak proudly told all that her son would be a hunter like his father.

"A great hunter," said Olson. "They will tell stories of this one."

That same day Morgan and Tiitaa walked off together and were gone a long time. I did not learn until later that Morgan had asked Tiitaa to go away with them, for as long as four seasons. Morgan said he needed a man he could trust. One good with the dogs. And one who could handle difficulties if they came.

Tiitaa gave Morgan's offer much consideration. He fell into a time of quiet, as our father often had, discussing his feelings only with Inuppak.

Morgan explained to Tiitaa that they were to meet two men in Foster's Bay. Then they would take the *North Wind* down the coast. They would help them set up a station and map a good part of the coastline. The *North Wind* would pick them up the following summer when the ice cleared.

For several days Tiitaa did not give Morgan an answer. Then, one evening when we were all gathered together, Tiitaa said to Morgan, "You are my friends. The two of you. And the only Qallunaat I truly respect and trust. And if you are in need of me, I will follow you. But my heart is here. With my wife and my son and my people. I wish never to go south again in this lifetime."

There was a second of silence. I could see the look of disappointment on Morgan's face and on Olson's. Then Morgan rested his hand on Tiitaa's shoulder. "A man should be where his heart is."

Tiitaa lifted Otek into his arms and held him there.

I saw a tear in Inuppak's eye as she looked at Tiitaa.

"We'll miss you not being with us," Olson told Tiitaa. "But Daniel is right. You should stay where your heart is. If I were half as smart as you, I'd be in Montreal. And after this job is over I'm going home to stay."

Morgan looked at Olson doubtfully but said nothing. Then he told Tiitaa they would be leaving in the morning. To get back to Foster's Bay while the snow was still good.

I felt a sudden emptiness in my heart at his words. It must have shown on my face, for I realized Inuppak was watching me.

Morgan said they would pick up supplies in Igloolik. It should be a good run from there.

"I'll go with you." I said it softly.

There was silence. They all looked at me with surprise. All but Inuppak, who appeared to expect it. I said it again. "I'll go with you."

"To Igloolik?" Morgan asked.

"No. South on the *North Wind.* I will go in Tiitaa's place."

There was still surprise on Morgan's face, and a touch of doubt. Tiitaa scratched his chin. He looked at Morgan. Morgan looked at him. One appeared to be questioning the other without offering a word.

"Well, we know she can handle a team of dogs," Olson said with a slight laugh.

I told them I could handle the dogs as well as

any of them. And keep a camp. I hunted and kept a camp with my father and he taught me to know the tundra. And work hard. "I know how to work hard." I didn't realize how excited my voice was. But I could see that Morgan was thinking about it. After a moment all were watching him. After a long moment of thought he shrugged his shoulders. He looked again at Tiitaa. Waiting for Tiitaa to say something. Finally Morgan said, "She's your sister."

But Tiitaa said nothing. He just looked at me thoughtfully.

Morgan turned to Olson. "We could definitely use someone to keep up the cabin. That would give us a lot more free time for mapping and research."

Olson nodded. "Why not? Hell, she's as much our sister too."

Morgan added. "And it would be a good thing to have another account of the expatiation. Maata can keep a journal of her own. She writes as well, or better than any of us."

"Agreed," said Olson.

We all turned to Tiitaa. Tiitaa was still doubtful. Then Inuppak leaned close and whispered into Tiitaa's ear. Tiitaa took her words seriously and thought about them for a long time. But he said nothing. Then I heard Inuppak say softly, "Maata has a hunger in her heart for new things and new places. She must be free for this just as you must be free to know the tundra. There are many different freedoms. Not all the same as yours. And to deny her these things would be to deny all that Nua wished for her. All that she is and can be in her own way."

After a moment Tiitaa nodded. "It is true." He looked at me and smiled. Turning to Morgan he said. "Yes. It should be."

Morgan turned to me. "Get your things together. We leave at dawn."

I jumped up and threw myself into Olson's big arms. Then I gave Morgan a hug. When I came to Tiitaa I embraced him warmly. He nodded his head in an understanding way. Then he passed little Otek into my arms. I looked at Otek's chubby face and knew I would miss him badly. His little hand reached for the amulet that hung from my neck.

Later, as I was gathering my things, Inuppak whispered, "Always know that we love you. That you have a place here when you are ready to return." Her voice was warm and sincere. But even as she spoke, I realized that I would never return to stay. I did not belong with Tiitaa and his people, just as I did not belong with those in Quebec City. I would need to find my own place and time. And at that moment I knew they were waiting for me to discover them.

And I still believe that I will discover them.

July 17

Last night I thought I lost Morgan. He was so still and quiet in his sleep, I didn't think he was breathing. Then I laid my hand on his arm, and after a time he moved slightly. And then his breathing was heavy again.

July 18

Rain. Cold and hard on the roof of the cabin, but it cleared as the morning passed away. For a long time I watched the hawk hunting along the shore, riding smoothly on the wind.

We met Frank Nicolson and Avery Smith in Foster's Bay only a few days before we were to go south on the *North Wind*. They had gear with them and also had credit at the Bay Company store. Morgan got the supplies we needed from the Bay store while Olson and I traded off a few of our huskies for new ones to strengthen our team.

The day before we were ready to leave, the morning the *North Wind* came into the bay, the Reverend Moorehead came to see me. He was amazed at the way I had grown. At the height I had gained. "You're almost a woman," he said. And he added that most Inuit girls my age would be married to some young hunter. But I told him I was not ready to marry. My words appeared to please him, and he told me I was too young, and far too bright, to waste my life away on the tundra.

"I don't think it would be wasted," I said. "But I'm not ready to marry."

He drew back a little. Then he offered in a most honest way, "Would you like to walk up to the cemetery? There is a place there for your father and mother. I thought you might like to go."

I looked at him strangely.

"I know," he said. "They did not recover them after they were lost on the ice. But still, there should be something to mark their passing."

So that morning we went up to the top of the hill

that looked out over Foster's Bay. The cemetery had grown to about a dozen graves, and each was marked with a small white cross. Reverend Moorehead and I stopped before two crosses. He stood with me a moment, and when I turned I realized he had drifted away to leave me on my own.

I am not sure my mother would have cared for the cross that marked her place. But I thought it was good that there was something, even though I knew her spirit wasn't there. And it was the same with my father. Though I remembered how Father loved to sing in the little church to the sound of the drum. And how we could hear his voice through the darkest night.

I did not speak to them on the hill that morning but only remembered them. I would speak to them in my time and way. When my words were carried by the wind.

Close by was Lisi's grave. And near to that was Siaja's. Four places I knew on the hill.

I held the amulet tight in my hand as I stood before Siaja. The woman who had given me words.

Moorehead returned beside me. He whispered a Christian prayer. "Our Father who art in heaven ..."

He went on, but my mind did not listen.

A moment later he touched my arm, and we

were moving down the hill together, with Foster's Bay and the ocean below. With the *North Wind* waiting on the water. "I have always been sorry for not listening to Krakoluk on that terrible day. I should never have pushed him to take the boat out. And there is seldom a moment when I don't think about it," Reverend Moorehead told me. But he also believed there is a reason for all things that happen to us in this life. And often he thought it was meant to fall on him to send me off to school in Quebec City. Then he asked softly if it was a good place. "I was told Mrs. Colville's was a good place," he said. He didn't want me taken away to one of those government-run boarding schools where they send other Inuit children. Where they try to change them.

I told him it was a good place.

"I believed I owed that to Krakoluk and Nua," he said.

I told him they tried to give me a Christian name.

"What was it?"

"Sarah."

"A beautiful name."

"But I don't use it."

We stopped walking for a moment. And he

said that perhaps I should keep it anyway. The world begins in the place where we are born, but it doesn't end there. It only begins.

"Father said that the wind blows to the end of the earth and comes back again."

"Then I believe it," said Reverend Moorehead. "I was foolish to doubt him once. And I believe his is the daughter of the wind. And the world your journey."

We were walking again. And we said nothing. I did not give a kind word to Reverend Moorehead that day, though I know he was searching for one. That was his loss, and now mine. But I had nothing to give him.

July 20

My father told me that the wind blows to the end of the earth and comes back again.

Nicolson tried to catch it. In the little cups he tied to the pole, he tried to measure it. They are still there, lonely, where he went each day. Each day marking down in his book what he read from them. But he must have read very little. Or did not understand what the wind was saying. Or he did not know how to listen.

I tried to warn Nicolson when he said he was leaving. And Morgan tried to tell him. But all he said was, "I'm not staying in this hut through the black winter with our supplies gone. The four of us can't live on what we salvaged from the fire."

Morgan said he had a better chance by staying. But Nicolson shook his head stubbornly. He was making a run for Seal Bay. There was no talking him out of it.

"And I'm going with him," Avery Smith said.

Nicolson faced Smith. "I'm not sure I want you along," he told him.

Smith drew up his chest angrily. He adjusted his glasses in that way of his and in a loud voice told Nicolson that two men had a far better chance of making it. And I remember the look between them. Each having little respect for the other.

"You would only be more weight for the dogs," said Nicolson.

"You need me," Smith repeated.

Finally Morgan held up his hand for quiet. He looked at Nicolson. "Take him with you," he said. It was like an order, but it was said easily.

Nicolson hesitated. He mumbled. Then agreed.

Daniel Morgan looked at me. "Do you agree,

Maata?" He asked it as an honest question.

I told him I did. But they were wrong for leaving.

Smith removed his glasses. His angry look fixed on me. He demanded to know what I had to do with it.

Morgan told him flatly that I had as much to do with it as he did.

Smith swelled with anger. Then Morgan turned to Nicolson. He told Nicolson he should wait a few days and cross over the sea ice.

"Wait for what?" Nicolson said.

Morgan looked at me again. "You tell them, Maata. This is your land."

I studied both of them. "The wind is blowing too hard," I said. "When it comes across the tundra like this, it can come for days without stopping." I told them the wind could tear the snow free and change the land. It could freeze a man on a running team. And it could blind you. People here know how to listen to the wind, I said. And they know how to wait.

They were both quiet. Then Smith said to Nicolson in a worried voice, "Maybe the girl is right."

Nicolson shook his head. And then he told

Smith in few words that if he was going, he should get some gear ready and help with the dogs. Then Nicolson threw on his heavy parka and went out to the team.

Smith put on his parka and started for the door. Before going out he turned to face us. He said they would send back help. "I promise," he said. Then he said it again. "We'll send help." He sounded a little guilty and very worried.

I remember Daniel Morgan's words to him. "A man shouldn't promise things he doesn't yet have."

Smith looked at both of us silently. Then he pulled the door closed going out.

July 21

One day long ago, one of those warm spring days that fall so pleasantly on Quebec like a gift, Celeste and I sat under a tree above the river. And I remember Celeste reading from a little book of poems. And one verse by William Cullen Bryant stayed in my mind.

> *Loveliest of lovely things are they*
> *On earth, that soonest pass away;*
> *The rose that lives its little hour*

219

Is prized above the sculptured flower;
Even love, long tried, and cherished long,
Becomes more tender and more strong
At thought of that insatiate grave,
From which its yearnings cannot save.

I got Mrs. Colville's letter from the Bay Company store on the same day we left Foster's Bay on the *North Wind*. Celeste, she wrote, died in February. She came down with a fever on a day of bitter cold and heavy snow. Old John went into the village for the doctor, but she was gone by the time he arrived.

She never liked the winter chill, I thought. She hated walking in the deep snow.

I folded the letter in my hand and leaned against the railing of the *North Wind*. My tears were cold on my face and my heart was as dark as the ocean below.

Celeste, Siaja, and Lisi. My mother and my father. My gentle Olson. All gone away from me.

Someday I will give them words. And put those words in books. For books are spirit things. Not all I've known is lost.

July 22

And it ends here.

This morning I went up on the hill and put new flowers on Olson's grave. Then I went on over the hill, out of sight of the cabin. When I heard the single blast of the shotgun shatter the still air, my heart stopped. I raced back up the hill as fast as I could. I had just reached the top when the second shot came. And there below I saw Morgan dragging himself away from the cabin to the water's edge. He loaded the gun and fired another shot. And there, out on the bay, was the *Venture*. She had dropped two small boats that were moving in toward the shore.

Morgan again fired off the shotgun. He was calling me back.

They are taking Morgan down to the boat now, and I will follow.

⌐ Author's Note ⌐

In January 1998, at a ceremony on Parliament Hill in Ottawa, the government of Canada formally pledged to support native self-government.

In April 1999 the Inuit were granted their own territory, an area where they will govern themselves under their own laws and customs. This new territory was named Nunavut—"our land."

⌐ Bibliography ⌐

Baffin Island, Northwest Territories, Arctic Canada, Northwest Territories Department of Economic Development and Tourism.

Briggs, Jean L. *Never in Anger, Portrait of an Eskimo Family,* Harvard University Press.

Bruemmer, Fred. *Arctic Memories, Living With the Inuit,* Key Porter Books, Toronto.

Dorais, Louis-Jacques. *Quaqtaq, Modernity and Identity in an Inuit Community,* University of Toronto Press.

Merck Manual of Medical Information, The. Merck Research Laboratories.

Mowat, Farley. *Sea of Slaughter,* Bantam Books.

National Geographic Magazine, *A Dream Called Nunavut,* September 1997 Issue.

Petrone, Penny, ed. *Northern Voices, Inuit Writing in English,* University of Toronto Press.

Van Nostrands Scientific Encyclopedia, fourth ed. D. Van Nostrand Company, Inc.